Threads of
TRUTH

Patrick Piccolo

Threads of TRUTH

Five Short Stories Exploring Faith

Tate Publishing & *Enterprises*

Threads of Truth
Copyright © 2011 by Patrick Piccolo. All rights reserved.

No part of this publication may be reproduced, stored in a retrieval system or transmitted in any way by any means, electronic, mechanical, photocopy, recording or otherwise without the prior permission of the author except as provided by USA copyright law.

This novel is a work of fiction. Names, descriptions, entities, and incidents included in the story are products of the author's imagination. Any resemblance to actual persons, events, and entities is entirely coincidental.

The opinions expressed by the author are not necessarily those of Tate Publishing, LLC.

Published by Tate Publishing & Enterprises, LLC
127 E. Trade Center Terrace | Mustang, Oklahoma 73064 USA
1.888.361.9473 | www.tatepublishing.com

Tate Publishing is committed to excellence in the publishing industry. The company reflects the philosophy established by the founders, based on Psalm 68:11,
"The Lord gave the word and great was the company of those who published it."

Book design copyright © 2011 by Tate Publishing, LLC. All rights reserved.
Cover design by Lauran Levy
Interior design by Nathan Harmony

Published in the United States of America

ISBN: 978-1-61777-054-8
1. Fiction: Short Stories
2. Fiction: Religious
11.02.08

Dedicated to Grandma Piccolo and Grandma Toth
In loving memory of James Timbers

Acknowledgments

Although I am young, my life has been incredibly blessed, not only in what I have experienced, but in whom I have had the privilege to know—and it is those people who have truly shaped my heart, molded my character, and touched my life in the most beautiful ways as to influence my writing and passions.

First and foremost, I have to acknowledge my family in its entirety, ranging from my grandparents, to my parents, to my amazing sister and all of my cousins. The best memories I have are from my childhood, taking the drive up to Pennsylvania for holidays or even just random trips during the summer. Pennsylvania has become a common setting for many of my stories, especially *Those Last Few Moments*. I still remember those summer days, running down to the cemetery with my cousin Sal Neri and playing volleyball with everyone at family picnics. I remember spending the night at my aunt Jane's, swimming in her pool and sleeping on their trampoline with Raynelle and Anna.

I remember family vacations, wanting to be just like my cousin Chris Smith and playing Uno at my great aunt Eleanor's. I remember going to my aunt Barbie's, joking around with my favorite little cousins Nicole, Mary, Cassandra, and Julie. Those are the moments in our childhood that seem so routine but perish with time, surviving only as the heart of our memories, the prize of our past. And it is that past that led me to where I am today and serves as an inspiration for my writing.

The glue of my mom's side of the family was my grandpa Toth. Grandpa Toth has probably had one of the greatest impacts of any one person on my life. From when he was alive, I remember the smell of his cigar smoke, the goofiness of his jokes, and the simplicity of his lifestyle. Grandpa was an icon in our family, and when he died, in many ways things seemed to fall apart. Still, in his death, I learned many things. I began to see his life beyond the lawn chair in his garage and began to realize how each person is a story—how at one point my grandpa was me, and one day I will be him. I saw my mom cry, which induced more pain than anything else yet showed me how a tragedy can serve as an adhesive to bring people together. I learned how even a tragedy can in some ways be a blessing. These are ideas that have strong places in many of my stories' themes.

I must also thank my parents. I could not have ever asked for a better set of parents than Ben and Sue Piccolo. Strict but encouraging, my parents have endorsed every dream I have ever had—which is a lot! They have been grounded and helped to keep me so, but never suppressing and always serving as my most passionate supporters in baseball, school, writing, or anything else. When I was younger, my dad never let me win, ever! Board games, basketball, ping pong, nope! If I was going to win, I had to earn it. This is the most valuable lesson I have been taught. Hard work is the only road to some point of achievement, and in fact, the journey through hard work, whether the goal is ultimately achieved, is some mark of success.

My mom always, *always*, encouraged me to dream—and so I did, and so I attempted to publish this book. If I could synthesize my mom and dad into one person, that is exactly who I would want to be.

My sister is one of my best friends and has always been a role model. She has a tender heart, filled with compassion, a brilliant mind, and much integrity. She has always been there for me, and she, too, has played an integral part in my journey leading to the publication of this book.

Thank you, Valerie Odell. I have read to Val everything I have written, ever since my freshman year in high school. She has always had an unrelenting faith in me and all that I do, and I am sure that this faith will continue to encourage me. Val is an absolutely amazing girl who has been one of the greatest lights in my life. I like to see every person as a story, and in mine, she has been one of the most powerful and impactful characters, hopefully willing to share her beauty with me for several chapters to come. I also want to give very special thanks to her brother, Andrew Odell, and her parents, Carol Elias and Mark Odell, for the impact all of you have had on me.

Thank you as well to Richard Elias and little Isabel; your interactions served as inspiration to me for the incredible love that exists between a father and his young daughter.

I want to thank Bob and M.J. Favilla, who served as role models and, more importantly, endorsers of my dreams. I used to talk to MJ for hours every day after school when I would go to her house to walk her dog, and these have become some of my fondest memories. I recall coming home from school and always being extremely eager to walk Max and later Rocky (her dogs). She has the most wonderful heart I have ever seen, the most unfailing optimism, the most outstanding compassion, and the most incredible personality. MJ Favilla shaped me by believing in me and showed me how a Christian should live.

All of my teachers, especially Mrs. Allison Alison, Mr. Al Faraone, Mr. Kevin McGuire, Mrs. Jo Ellen Sholl, and Mrs. Sara Sturtz, should be thanked. Each has changed my life in some huge way, and I could not be more blessed to have had them, not only as teachers, but as mentors. Mrs. Alison has more empathy than anyone you will meet; Mr. Faraone, Mrs. Sholl, and Mrs. Sturtz, all English teachers, had such a passion for literature that it fostered the same enthusiasm in me. And Mr. McGuire, though a *math* teacher, is one of the most outstanding role models I have.

Mr. and Mrs. Adams, Josh Haltom, and my high school youth group, including Caleb Adams, Nate and Kyle Ostrander: these people changed my life and taught me about Christ. The love I received from them is immeasurable, and I can't say enough. Even now, as I progress in my new Bible studies, I still quote many things Josh told me.

Coach Sam Plank, Coach James Timbers, Coach Sean Griffin, Coach Jason Treon, and my entire high school baseball team. Baseball has always been one of my greatest passions, and this coaching staff, along with all of my teammates, have given me some of my most cherished experiences. Coach Plank and the rest of this team did not just help me evolve as a baseball player but even more so as a person.

My younger neighbors Sean and Joel Friedman—when faced with pressure from those around me to engage in un-Christian behavior, I have lived for these two boys. I want to be someone they can look up to and be proud of, and they have unknowingly guided my life.

Next, all of the incredible friends who have touched my life, including Taylor Tice, Ryan Robles, Matt Miscione, T.J. O'Neal, and John Karasinski. Taylor Tice, my roommate and my best friend: I cannot acknowledge him enough for how unbelievable a friend he is and how he has changed my life. Ryan Robles—I have never had such a bond with any one person in my life. Ryan and I have shared many common struggles and worked through them with each other, and he is truly a brother to me. We have had some of the most powerful conversations and really grown in Christ together. Matt has always been there, for anything and everything, and T.J. and John have each been remarkable friends.

And thank you, Brittany Harton, for taking the time to read these stories, give honest feedback, and engage in intellectual conversation about their themes.

Thank you to the entire Tate Publishing family for your hard work, passion, and cooperation in helping to publish this book.

Most importantly, thank you, Jesus Christ, for giving me patience in producing this book and for blessing my life with the people who surround me every day.

This book is not my product, but rather it is a product of all of these people and how they have molded my life.

Table of Contents

The Willow Tree
~ 15 ~

Hidden Temple
~ 30 ~

The Rocket Man
~ 54 ~

In the Darkness
~ 69 ~

Those Last Few Moments
~ 93 ~

The Willow Tree

It is amazing to me, the stories you will hear if you just stand still. Just listen. Listen to the way the birds sing songs into the wind; listen to the way the water softly swishes through the creek and to the way the thunder rumbles against the clouds. There is a story in everything—every piece of life, every fragment of time, every emotion, every breath. Stories define the walls of life, they mold the boundaries of time, and they are all mixed together, simultaneously jumbled into the complexity of a second—but still, they reconcile perfectly.

Listening is all I can do. Listen and watch. I have been in the same place for sixty years, dripping over the shoulders of multiple generations, hearing, reading their stories. For the most part, these stories have been conventional—although every story is special—they were still, should I say, not surprising. That was true until Timothy Lucinder moved into the house that was built beside my roots.

You see, I am a Weeping Willow tree, and my story is only the recording of those lives I have witnessed. Timothy's story came to define my life.

He moved in when he was about eight years old, and his imagination transformed the world around me. Every child has dreams and hopes, but his were distinct. He had this deeper faith, deeper than the roots beneath my trunk, stronger than the trunk that supports my branches.

He would play war, play baseball, play doctor, and pretend that he was an animal, all beneath the careful observance of my swaying arms. But his life would then evolve from this innocence into something truly special—a kind of human perseverance unlike any I had ever seen.

Not every tree has the opportunity to witness what I saw in Timmy's life. Here is the story I was blessed to be a part of.

First there was Charlotte. She was a good girl—really adorable. When she was younger, she would pretend to be a princess. She would tie herself around my loose branches and make beautiful gestures to her adoring suitors across the creek. As she got older, she would write in her diary beneath the warm and careful watch of my branches.

She would carve her name in a heart, along with her first love's, into my thick bark. They are married now, and the carving is still there.

Then there was Billy. Billy would use branches as guns and find shelter behind my trunk. He would dance around me, defeating his enemy with his ruthless courage. He would go on to win a medal of honor.

But when both Charlotte and Billy grew up, their dreams stopped. They lost faith in the world that they invented in their backyards, and although they were eventually happy, their optimistic conviction and perception of the good in the world was eventually replaced with skepticism.

But then came Timmy. What made him special?

It wasn't anything he did. Just like any other child, his imagination changed the grass into clouds, the creeks into oceans, the birds into airplanes, stars into snowflakes in the middle of summer—eternally falling from heaven. Every kid has a dream world. It was more how he did it.

The first day he moved in, he ran into the backyard, his baby sister, just three years old, waddling behind him. He lived with his grandpa, and Amy was his younger and only sister's name.

This much I learned from move-in day and that night: he and his sister would be king and queen of the world...

"Amy! Amy, take that stick!"

Amy just giggled and picked up the stick.

"Now, Amy, that's your magic wand! You can do anything you want to with it!"

Amy swung the stick in circles.

"Whoa! Amy, did you just see that! You made the stars shoot across the sky!"

Amy's face dropped as she stared up at the open sky.

"Do it again, Amy!" Timmy cheered on his sister. He found a flower and stuck it behind her ear. "And now you're the most beautiful princess in all the land. You see that tree? You see its branches move? It is bowing down to you, Amy."

Amy just smiled. I doubt she knew what was going on, but Timmy saw everything so clearly. He found a stick himself and stabbed the ground.

"This is our land, Amy!"

And the dream continued into the night. Princess Amy and King Timmy. I never saw finer royalty.

A week later, Timmy was a baseball player. He came outside dressed in baseball pants, his dirtied Yankee shirt tucked in, and a dress belt (probably his grandpa's) hanging loose from his waist.

"Now batting, number sixteen, the great Timmy Lucinder!"

Holding a balled-up sock in one hand and a big wooden spoon in the other, Timmy stepped up to the plate.

"The pitch to Lucinder, and this one is swung on. Oh baby, it's deep! Look at this one go!"

The sock flew up into the wind and was carried into my rustling arms. Timmy sprinted around the backyard, simultaneously screaming as the birds chirped in approval.

"Lucinder did it again! Here he comes, flying around third. They're going to wave him in!"

Timmy slid hard against the dirt into the imaginary home plate. Safe.

The game, to my amazement, lasted hours. It was a joy to watch. If only I could speak... I wanted so badly to join him.

Threads of Truth

You can learn a lot about someone from their dreams, though. It is just an open imagination, pouring out hopeful possibilities. And hope was exactly what Timmy's life was founded on.

At the end of the game, he snuggled up against the base of my trunk. I felt his small body above my roots. I saw his spirit carry off into a further dream world of sleep.

He slept until his grandfather came out and carried him off into the house. Another successful day for Timmy Lucinder at the ballpark.

Timmy continued to dream and fantasize throughout his adolescence. One day I would be Mt. Everest, and then next I would find myself as a pyramid, roasting in the hot Egyptian desert. Each day brought about something new; each day there was a new destination, a new dream fostered.

Nothing was more exciting to me than to be included in the stories that so purely reflected the innocence of Timmy. I loved how he would inspire the imagination of Amy and even include his grandpa. He was a carrier of purity, a walking painting of untouched virtue.

Through his dreams, every day I learned more about my young hero. But one day he had a friend over, and a great shadow was lifted to shed light on his story.

Timmy's friend was named Taylor, and he was a great kid. Oh, what a great heart he had.

They had just finished playing baseball and were resting in the shade beneath my branches.

"Timmy," Taylor began, his eyes sparkling with innocence, "why don't you have a mom? Or a dad?"

I watched Timmy's eyes get really dark.

"My parents died in a car crash when I was younger."

"Oh…man."

It was quiet for a minute. The two just sat there, and I rested in shock. I suppose I should have seen it. Why else would he live with his grandfather?

Still, it was that ever green optimism that burned in everything he did. I couldn't imagine anyone being so buoyant and so hopeful with such a depressing history.

But I guess that was what made Timmy really special to me. After the silence passed, the two friends got up and proceeded to find joy in their dreams.

That's when it hit me. Sadness didn't last; pain didn't continue. No doubt it was real, and it was there—but hope was inherent. It wasn't thought about, but the future was beautiful, and that is just how it was. The sun would rise in the morning, and life would go on.

Amy became more and more endearing as she grew older, her soft smile and blue eyes as gentle as the smooth clouds that grazed against the sky. She was warm and compassionate for a young girl. And boy, did she look up to Timmy.

The two would play for hours, dancing around me, prancing and skipping through the garden. Two breaths of innocence, sweeping across the backyard.

Timmy also grew older and maintained his enthusiasm; however, at the age of twelve he had his first girlfriend.

Her name was Alyssa. She had silky brown hair, misty green eyes, and good posture; but behind her youthful elegance lay the same playful spirit as was in Timmy. They sat beneath my weeping branches and stared up at the moving clouds, the star-lit skies, the melting sunset—whatever scenery God draped across the heavens.

Puppy love is so beautiful. It is just so innocent and pure, like childhood itself. It saddened me to think of when they would grow up and life would scar their untainted spirits. I worried that with their loss of innocence, there would be a loss of optimism, a loss of hope. Loss of hope is the scariest thing on earth. It is the loss of life.

Nonetheless, the days carried on, and Alyssa came and went. Timmy grew up, and high school came. As if his story hadn't already captured my heart, it was in the years that followed the age of fifteen that would really do me in. I saw that Timmy was this very special person, more different than anyone else, more so than I could have imagined.

If there is a time when I saw innocence corrupted it was late middle school and high school. Timmy was no exception. He was not sheltered in any way from this experience.

When he was fifteen, he had his first kiss, right beside my trunk. When he was sixteen, he had his first drink, and he eventually spit it all back up, right upon my roots. When he was seventeen, he smoked a joint, and the smoke suffocated my branches. All the parts of me that had witnessed his innocence now witnessed his equal impurities.

I took it as it was—growing up. He was still a good kid; not that I condone these things, but oh, his heart was still so pure, his compassion still so colorful, his grace still so relentless. Amy was just reaching the pinnacle of her childhood, and Timmy was bringing an effective close to his. However, even with this whole growing-up ordeal, the dark cynicism I had seen obscure the perspective of all those before him never showed up. I wondered if it would. My answer would come when he turned eighteen.

Caroline Jacquelyn Brecher moved to our small town when Timmy was a senior in high school. She was a smart gal and very good looking. Her eyes roared with white waves of beauty, ebbing against this fantastic blue ocean—a perfect blend of colors. Her hair was dark blonde, tied around splashes of brown; it hung from her head in strands of silk, like dark braids of gold. Timmy gave her one look, and he was gone.

They went on their first date two weeks after she moved in, and within months they were that small town's favorite couple. They went for long walks, shared long talks, and became obsessed with each other. I didn't think much of it; I heard them share their first "I love yous" and kisses. It was romantic, but I still thought of it as puppy love, until I realized one night just how grown-up Timmy had become.

Caroline and he sat underneath my long, swaying arms, gazing at the stars as the heavens stared back down through the moon. Caroline reached over to grab his hand, and slowly the night unfolded until it peaked in explosions of lust.

Two months later, Caroline found that she was pregnant.

"We can't keep it!"

"Timmy, we have to. I can't kill it. I can't do it."

"But it was a mistake. We have to. What are we going to do? I mean, what about school and everything? Our future is gone."

"Maybe our future is being born."

"Caroline, are you kidding me? We are frickin' eighteen, nineteen years old, this...we...we just can't. I can't do this."

"I'm keeping the baby, Timmy."

The argument grew and carried on, and tears followed. I tried to soak up his salty pain, I tried to reach for his heart with one of my long arms, but nothing moved except when my aging branches would lift and fall in the wind. I wondered what would happen. What would happen to the baby? To Timmy? How would his grandfather take it?

But mostly I worried about Timmy and his optimism. I looked to see if his joy would cripple beneath his mistake.

This didn't happen. He told his grandfather, and the old man tried not to be mad. Timmy quit school, he got a job, and he prepared to adjust his life, but still he moved forward, never stopping to sulk, simply letting the tide of time carry his life to some eventual future.

Caroline had the baby seven months later, and his name was Jacob.

Jacob was the most beautiful thing I could have ever seen. It is crazy how something can seem so tragic—a mistake, a sin, an error, and then turn into the most wonderful blessing. Suddenly the baby was no longer a passionate night; it was a breathing life, with a heart, a soul, a mind, and a future.

And so life moved forward for Timmy. He did not marry Caroline, but he continued to support his young son. He was there for his first smile, his first step, his first dirty diaper. He worked as a mechanic at a local car shop and made enough money to pay for Jacob's expenses.

Amy, too, grew up and went to college, on track to become a doctor.

That would have been Timmy had it not been for Jacob, but still, he was happy, and life went on with hope of a better future still lingering in his heart.

Jacob started school at the age of five, and by that point, Timmy was hoping to return to night school, perhaps with the chance of getting a better office job. He drove Jacob to school every morning.

Jacob was just like his dad: big heart, big dreams, eternal optimism. He would come over to play in his great-grandfather's backyard. I watched him play the same games Timmy had beneath my branches; I saw his imagination pour out in its most pure forms. I saw the same innocence dance around, and occasionally I would see that purity reborn in Timmy. Two generations, one in the midst of adolescence, the other enduring the painful struggles of young adulthood.

"He is a great kid." Timmy's grandpa entered their world of imagination one day.

"I know," Timmy responded with a smile. Both had their eyes fixed on Jacob as his heart and imagination raced around my old trunk. Like Grandpa, I too was nearing the end of my time.

"A real blessing."

"I know."

"How is Caroline?"

"She is surviving. I think she met someone, so she is moving along."

"Really? That's great to hear. How about you? How are you doing?"

"I'm thinking about going back to school. I am tired of the grease; I want a job that I can make a difference with, you know. Change the world."

"Yeah." Timmy's grandpa smiled. "I know one world that you change and impact every day."

"Yeah." Timmy chuckled and returned the smile.

I don't know how to explain it, but somehow I felt this moment was very special. Jacob lived his dreams out through his play, with reality in front of him, as Timmy chased the dreams he hoped to live, reality trapping him, and their grandfather watched the two of them with a heart of wisdom, understanding everything, with a lifetime of living and chasing behind him.

And all the while the world spun round and time moved on. The past constantly building, the present constantly changing and planning, and the future staring back at the present, laughing at those plans, all knowing how it will play out. The only thing constant in it all is that the world continues to spin, lungs continue to breathe, and the sun continues to rise and fall.

After their visit, Timmy and Jacob left to go to Caroline's house. She had moved in with the man she met, and things were getting serious.

They got in their car seats and buckled in. Timmy slowly backed out of the driveway. He turned on his lights and headed down the dark road.

Music blasted from the radio, and Jacob danced and sang along. Timmy smiled and watched the road. They continued down the street up to the stop light. It was red as they approached, but as they reached the light it turned green, and Timmy accelerated into the intersection.

Out of nowhere a pick-up truck rammed full speed into the side of their car and sent them spinning. They twisted across the intersection, and the pick-up truck turned over and skidded to a stop on its side.

Great lights flashed, horns roared into the night, and Timmy's car rolled to a stop. I watched from the backyard, my sight ranging just over the small one-story houses that decorated the street. A shiver of shock cracked my trunk from roots to branch.

Sirens came soon after. Somehow I knew the night was only destined for tragedy from there on.

Amazingly, Timmy survived. The collision cast him through the air and gravity slammed his head against the road; a spray of crimson blood was caught in a sudden gust of wind. Timmy's eyes moved through the night in search of his wrecked car, and his son. But suddenly, a burst of light and a blast of heat divided the darkness

Threads of Truth

as flames consumed the vehicle and the small body that remained locked inside its tragic chambers. Timmy's body was spread across the open road, shards of shattered glass reflecting the blazing fire. A slow moment of realization, and a loud cry echoed from his broken heart. He prayed to drown beneath his tears.

The night grew dark and carried its ominous grief into the following day through the hearts of Timmy, Caroline, and the entire town.

It was more than the death of a boy. It was the death of a son, a great-grandson, a future, a set of dreams, a collection of hopes, an emblem of innocence and purity. And the next time I saw Timmy, I thought it was the death of him. I thought he would have lost all optimism, all hope, all faith. He had lost his father, his mother, and his son to car accidents, and through all of them he had survived.

The next time I did see him was six months later, and he sat at the base of my trunk. Tears covered his face and drowned his heart.

"Oh this tree," he began. "You are the only thing that has always been here. Day after day, dream after dream, sunrise, sunset, your roots never leave the solid ground. Somehow you are always watching." He paused and sobbed for a few moments. "*Why?*" His cries echoed through my branches, which for the first time truly wept from my core.

"Why?" he continued. "Why did I live? Why did they die? How is this fair? I made her pregnant, and I quit school. I restructured my life to prepare for his coming. I lived for him. He became the center of my life, the center of my heart." He paused again.

"And now, now it's as if he was not born five years ago. He is dead! He's gone! O God! How is this fair? How is it possible? My life is just here now, no purpose, no point. My prayers are dangling in the wings of hopelessness. Why should I live? Why do you keep me here? I don't see how you can put my life here and challenge me. I always had faith, I never doubted life or God or anything. I've done nothing to bring this upon myself, and now all I ask for is to trade places with my son. Let him have a shot at this whole thing."

The sky opened up, the clouds parted, and the stars gleamed down. The world went round, and the night moved on.

"It doesn't make sense, does it, tree? It is just how it is, how it is meant to be. We can't understand the plan, and we are not supposed to. We just keep this blind faith and live out this phony joy, hoping, always hoping, that someday it may become real. But it never does. We just chase and chase and chase, but our dreams are like the future they are contained in, always in front of us, never with us, except for in childhood. Jacob is dead, but the world will go on, and I am still here for some reason. We think we know the plan, we think we have it worked out, but then it is all gone, just like that. And so we believe, in moments of grief, that there is no plan. But there is." The tears began to dry.

"It just isn't our plan. There is a plan, we just don't know it; we can't know it. We just have to live it out. We just have to trust life and trust that somehow, every turn our story takes, there will be resolution. There will be real happiness. Our road may be broken, it may be shattered, but if we stay straight, if we let time take control of our lives, all will resolve. We can't ever lose faith and must always have hope, because God has laid the tracks of our lives, and in the story of a lifetime, a month, a year, a decade may be nothing, and it may be everything. But the point is, we don't know. Life is a surprise. All there is to do is live and be happy, because no matter what, the world will go round, and time won't stop."

He stood up and stared straight ahead at the distant horizon. Optimism again filled his eyes. No doubt a deep, mournful sadness clouded his vision, but behind it was that same faith that had been and, I came to see, would always be there.

Timmy was a special person. No, he was more than a special person. He lived his whole life in a giant childhood, with hope inherent to his heart. And so he walked into the night with no plan in his hand, just trust in the tracks that had been laid in front of him. One step, one day at a time, he lived his life. Meanwhile I continued to grow old and slowly felt the inevitable begin to press on my aging roots.

And all the while, God stared down and paved the road of time, complete with struggles, twists, turns, speed bumps, and construction zones; our lives in one hand and in his other, the world continued to go round.

Hidden Temple

The earth is so beautiful from the sky. No borders, no lines; just perfect and harmonious continuity. Easily the land becomes water and the water fades into land, an awesome blend of colors melting into each other.

It is peaceful. It is natural, without any apparent pattern, like a puzzle with pieces, but more whole. Just one entity, one body, the world as it had been created.

That's what I was thinking as I soared across the country and the ocean, destined for the Middle East. I am an archaeologist, and I was studying ancient Israel. I had been up on my reading and research but had yet to actually visit the "holy" land. I was travelling with my dear friend and fellow archaeologist, Andrea. She also happened to be my wife of six years.

We have no kids. Both my parents have been dead since I was sixteen, and my faith in God had died with them, lost in the same fires of that fatal car accident. But that was okay. It was sixteen years later, and I was doing just fine. Faith is phony. It is some false coat of security that "spirituals" drape across their heart. I didn't need that. I had true strength; I had character.

Still, I couldn't help but feel like this journey to Jerusalem should have some spiritual value. At least Andrea thought it did.

The flight was long but beautiful. We flew first into Frankfurt, then to Rome, and finally to Jerusalem. I slept for most of the flight, taking small intervals to look out through the window and enjoy the sights. Up there in the sky is the only time we get to see the world without nations—it is simply life, time, continuous like the land itself.

We got off the plane at one in the morning on a Saturday, and, being the middle of July—although there the weather is fairly unchanging—it was mildly hot. A Muslim taxi driver transported us from the airport to our hotel, which was only a ten-minute bus ride from our study site. Andrea and I carried our luggage up two flights of stairs, where we found our old, dirty room. Dust draped the walls, and mosquitoes threatened an aerial attack at any point during the night.

Still we managed to fall asleep, needing to be well rested before the first day of what would become, unexpectedly, the longest week of our lives.

In any case, the next morning Andrea and I woke up and snagged breakfast in the hotel lobby. We caught a cab to the study site, and there we met Ben Fergusson, the director of American Archaeological Operations.

"Nick! Good to see you, big guy," Ben began in his deep, booming voice. He was a big man, about six foot four, maybe two hundred sixty pounds. A thin mustache decorated his upper lip, and a receding hairline hid beneath a dirtied, old Red Sox hat.

"Hey, Ben. I've been good. Glad to finally make it out here. You know Andrea, right?"

"Of course! Nice to have you here also, Andrea. So what're you guys up to?"

"Well," Andrea cut in, "we are doing a study on Israeli history with special focus on the construction and destruction of the ancient temple that Solomon built."

"Oh, that's right. Well, I've got a site over here that should have some interesting material." Ben pointed toward the east, where a small plot of dirt remained untouched. Small pieces of stone broke the ground and hinted at hidden mysteries just a dig away.

"Has it been worked on at all?"

"No, sir. Any mystery is yours to discover, but no promises. The temple has a pretty shadowed history."

"Well, I guess that is the point of my job, to search the shadows for what is otherwise unseen." All three of us shared a quick, un-heartened laugh.

Ben may seem like a nice guy, and he really isn't bad. I had attended school with him in Pennsylvania years earlier, but he was always a bit arrogant. He always seemed to act as if he were above the world, his strut pushing his chin and ego high into the clouds. Still, we pretended to get along, and, needless to say, I was excited about this dig.

Andrea and I got straight to work. Shovels in hand, brushes in pocket, and excitement on our faces, we delicately attacked the land. We searched for hours and uncovered what appeared to be a small stone house, but it was absolutely bare. Not a single find, no mark of encouragement, no sign of life at all.

"Hey, Ben, come here."

Ben went into a slow trot, a swagger in even his jog.

"What's up?"

"What is this land supposed to be?"

"You tell me. I thought that was your job." A smirk worked across his face.

"But we are supposed to be uncovering artifacts about Solomon, the temple, David even. Something to help our research. It looks like a peasant or a servant lived here maybe."

"Treasures can be found in the most unexpected places, Nick."

"Yeah, but I prefer to search the expected places first. Now, shouldn't I be on top of the mountain, perhaps where the temple was built?"

"Nick, the temple was destroyed in the sixth century B.C.E. What do you expect to find? It was even rebuilt and destroyed again. You will work in vain."

"I don't care. *This* is in vain. Take me to Mount Zion."

"C'mon, Nick, I'm sure you know as well as anybody that people still debate where the temple was built. It was destroyed two thousand six hundred years ago, almost. There is no way to tell."

"Well, take me somewhere. We should go past the Zion gate, where the tomb of David is. Perhaps we can find something to help our study."

"Big guy, that is a tourist zone, not a site for archaeological study."

"Then we will go as informed tourists."

"Maybe tomorrow. It is getting late. The sun will go down in a few hours. Why don't you just keep searching this site for now?"

Disheartened, I turned back to the stone house.

Soon after, Andrea and I pulled ourselves from the site of our digging and went out to dinner. We drove across Jerusalem and found a nice, traditional Middle Eastern restaurant. We got two orders of Shish Taouk (basically chicken kebobs) and ate beneath the sunset.

Behind the mountains that lined the western borders of the city, the sun melted across the horizon. It disintegrated and cast out its final bursts of light into the sky, a final breath of beauty before the stars came out from hiding.

"There is something out there," I began. I took a bite of my kebob and tasted the tender meat. "There is a mystery out there, Andrea, and we are going to discover it."

Andrea laughed and looked out at the horizon. "There is something out there, Nick. The question is, will it be what you are looking for?"

The day faded into night with the gentle wind that swept across the city. We went back to the room and fell asleep.

In the morning the sun rose and stretched its bright fingers through our window, illuminating the room. Andrea and I sprung from bed and prepared for the day—it was a big one. We headed down to the hotel lobby, where we met Ben at eight o'clock to head out to the tomb of David.

Ben drove a worn-out van, the paint chipped all along the side, the inside leather torn and stained. I sat in the front passenger seat, and Andrea hopped in the back as we drove through the streets of Jerusalem.

"So what do you know about the temple of Solomon?" I asked Ben.

"I know it was built, and the Israelites and Judeans saw it as the throne of God, sitting on top of the Cosmic Mountain, where the divine met the mortal. They thought it was inviolable, especially during the time of the prophet Isaiah, but Jeremiah came with a new message just before Nebuchadnezzar and the Babylonians captured the city and Yahweh's throne in the early sixth century B.C.E. Under the Babylonians, it was destroyed, though later rebuilt after the exile, during the reign of Cyrus the Great and the new Persian power." Ben smiled and quickly shot a look toward the passenger side, sharing his smirk also with Andrea through the rear-view mirror. "I'm sure nothing you didn't already learn in your research."

"Yeah, and they rebuilt it. Um, did they rebuild it in the same place as the original?"

"Yes, but that was also later destroyed by the—"

"By the Romans," interrupted Andrea from the back seat.

"Very good." Ben smiled.

We headed south of the city and drove along a tattered road, barely squeezing through the Zion Gate, approaching the tomb of King David. Ben rolled to a stop near the infamous king's resting place. He let us go, gave us some last-minute advice and instruction, and then proceeded to wheel back into the main city.

Tourists flocked all around, as it obviously was not an established archaeological site; still, it was better than what we had been working with—at least we were on the holy ground. Andrea and I scouted the area, first indulging our curiosity in David's actual tomb. It was highly decorated in blue cloths, covered with ancient Hebrew symbols, and tile formed the foundation of the memorial. I looked around at the walls that had been burnt from ancient fires, as David's tomb is located on the bottom floor of an old synagogue. It had later been taken under Christian control as a church—St. Mary's of Zion—and was even later used as a Mosque until the war of 1948, when the Jews won it back. It had fluidly moved under the control of each major monotheistic religion, changing with the tide of time, yet never losing its significance.

In that moment it occurred to me the magnitude of the history I searched through. At one time, that history had been the present. At one time, David had lived, breathed, and believed in this great God. He was ignorant to the future, holding on to some sliver of hope that comes naturally to all mankind, believing somehow that the future will one day be real. *And then it comes*, I thought, *and it passes, and it is all eventually history.*

Dust in the wind, a breath of life, and a blink of time washed away by the falling rain, dried up by the rising and setting sun. *One day*, I thought, *this day will be meaning-*

less, and I too will rest eternally in some tomb. History will preserve my name and my life in some bottle of time, only to be washed up against some forgotten shore.

"What do these symbols say?" Andrea asked, breaking the silence.

"I'm not sure, exactly. I'm guessing some sort of tribute to his kingship. Probably not too important." I gazed over the tomb one more time, but in my quick gaze, my eye caught a small hole behind the tomb. "What's that?"

"What's what?"

"Look there, the tomb is covering something. What is it?" I looked around to see if anyone was watching then reached across the tomb. I pulled it closer to me, only to unveil a small hole. "Look, Andrea, it's a hole."

"So?" Andrea chuckled. "The walls are old; of course there are holes."

"No, no, this means something." I spoke on some unconfirmed conviction. I pulled the tomb slightly closer to my chest.

"Nick! Stop that!" Andrea pleaded in a desperate whisper. I still continued to pull it a little closer. I finally was able to reach inside. My hand dug through cobwebs before finding the grip of what felt like a wedge or a handle.

"There is a lever here or something."

"Huh?" Andrea leaned over the tomb to get a look. She reached with her hand, and I guided her to our mystery knob. Her eyes lit up as she turned to see my equally excited face.

"Finding your way around all right, I see." A familiar voice gripped our ears.

"Ben, hey!" I said, turning. "Yeah, just feeling around."

"Well, there is nothing back there. This is where King David lies at rest, as you know. He was considered the greatest king in Israel's history. The anointed one, the chosen one, God's servant. He 'did what was right in the sight of the Lord.' A Jewish legend, of course, his body is not really in there. It is just a mark of respect—and hope, of course."

"Yes, of course. He is also the father of Solomon, the one who built the original temple. We have obvious interest."

"Yeah, well, I was coming to see if you all wanted a ride back into to town for some lunch. You can always come back later."

"Umm..." I glanced at Andrea. "Sure."

We left the tomb, but we had made a discovery, and we would be back.

We went to lunch at one of the only American joints in town. I got a burger, and Andrea had the same. Both of our thoughts were locked on our latest encounter behind David's tomb. If only we could turn that latch, I felt like I would be unlocking a world of secrets. I felt on the verge of discovery, the brink of greatness, and my heart had never clenched on to hope any tighter.

The truth is, in my years to that point I had been less than successful. I lacked the experience of any journey worth recounting. I had not made any great discoveries, started a book, nor did I have any idea of what I would write about. I had spent my entire life working for the moment in which opportunity would arise and possibility would lie in the quake of mystery.

Failure, however, plays tricks on your dreams. It challenges your faith in anything, teasing your hope. And well, I'd had my fair share, but when I wrapped my fingers around that latch, I discovered my hope had not disappeared, it had only faded behind layers of disappointment. I rediscovered excitement, unveiled my seemingly hidden faith in possibility, and I wasn't going to let go until I opened that unfamiliar door of opportunity—literally.

"You found something," Andrea whispered across the table with a gleaming smile.

"I know. We've got to go back there. I'm afraid we can't go when there are so many people around, though. We have to go some time later."

"There will always be guards. At least now it would be easier to get in, not to mention legal."

"I would rather try to deceive the two eyes of a lazy guard than the wide-open eyes of hundreds of tourists. Not to mention, the guards will be watching now too."

"Fair enough. Tonight?"

"Absolutely."

A childish energy fueled our plans as we told Ben we were going to another site instead of the tomb. He seemed too satisfied with our leaving the tomb to ask where we were going, and we left for Solomon's throne, where we would design our strategy.

Solomon's throne was beautiful and almost inspirational as we drew up our tactics. It was going to be an exciting adventure, and all I could think was that it was about time.

At about ten o'clock, Andrea and I found our way back to the Zion gate. Two security guards kept careful watch at the front entrance. Dressed in all black, we danced through the night, high on excitement and mystery and humbled only by the corresponding fear of danger. We managed to sneak by the front security with relative ease as the darkness swallowed our costumes. The real challenge was getting into the tomb, however.

We crawled and crept into the night until we met the entrance to the tomb. Andrea kept close watch of our surroundings as I sacrificed my secrecy upon my entry into the holy lair. Slowly, we softly stepped through the heavy black until we reached the tomb.

I took a deep breath and once again reached across the tomb. I felt for the knob that had ignited my enthusiasm earlier in the day, but for some reason could not locate the latch. I threw my hand in a ruthless panic against the wall but to no avail. It was as if it had disappeared! Then I heard a voice echoing down the hallways of the tomb, ricocheting off the ceiling and the dense walls, filling the darkness with fear.

Andrea and I quickly ducked behind the wall. The voice grew and grew, like a massive wave approaching the shores of uncertainty. But as it continued to grow, we also began to recognize it. It was Ben.

"Yes, I know, but they are very smart. We mustn't let them discover anything. Just keep the hole covered; I don't know how it became uncovered in the first place."

"But we cannot cover it tonight." Another voice, higher pitched and much softer, also hissed through the shadows.

"That's fine. But have it concealed by morning. I assure you, they will be back."

They faded into the night as they passed by. Andrea and I came out from our hiding and returned to the tomb. They had to be talking about our discovery from earlier. But why?

It was a puzzling question, but still my most threatening concern was that if it was not yet covered, why couldn't I find it now? I returned to reach across the tomb, racing my hand against the cold, dusty wall. Slowly, my hand worked its way into a small, familiar crevice. It was still there.

I reached in and prepared to pull.

"Wait!" Andrea gasped. "Are you sure we should do this?"

I just smiled. "I don't know. Let's find out."

With that, I pulled the latch. I heard a great shifting sound, like a massive boulder moving, but nothing happened. Just loud rumbling stomped through the hallways. I peered all around to find some newly opened door, but there was none. The noise was enough to draw our friends from earlier back toward the tomb. Startled by the charging footsteps, Andrea and I darted back into the night. We abandoned all strategy and dashed through the darkness, sprinting in search of some sort of safety. We eventually found it in a small cove of trees nearby.

We could hear the powerful voice of Ben bellowing into the wind, threatening the darkness to reveal its refugees. There was nothing for me and Andrea to do but wait. By early morning, adrenaline had kept our restless minds awake, and we found our way back into town. The thrilling night had led us in and out of danger but still without answers. We treaded in uneasy waters, but our questions would have to wait at least a day longer.

Later that morning, we met again with Ben. The initial confrontation was awkward. We could feel he knew about our adventures of the night before. His eyes carefully scanned our faces and seemed to stare into our very thoughts.

"Where to today?" Ben asked with a tone that emitted not only his traditional arrogance but also some other very awkward connotation. It was as if he were saying, "I know what you've been up to, and I'm on to it."

"The tomb of David," I answered squeamishly, submitting to his intimidating figure and voice.

"No can do. They are doing some special construction. Rumor is, someone broke in there last night."

Awkwardly I stared back at him. The moment twisted the air between us, and the atmosphere suddenly felt dense, heavy with unsaid accusations but also unspoken confessions.

"Well, then, I guess it is off to Solomon's throne again." Andrea stepped in to melt the moment that seemed frozen between us.

"All right, I can do that."

We spent the day under the observant eye of Ben, ravaging through Israel's history and the reign of Solomon. Every once in a while Andrea and I would share a quick glance, and we both knew that our adventure for the week was only beginning.

The first question we had to answer was why the door didn't open. And what was the rumbling? What had happened? I thought and searched through every book and surfed the Web in a frantic hunt for answers. I imagined the mechanics of the door, continually replaying the event that had occurred the night before. I rolled my eyes back and felt my hand wrap around the latch and twist, pull, turn. The lock popped; I remember that feeling in my hand. Then the powerful rumbling. Finally it hit me.

When I was younger, I had this small cube with a tiny, silver ball inside a maze that covered the cube's walls. It was a kind of safe with open space in the middle and a door on one side. The objective was to work the ball through the maze until it fell into this small crevice. You then pushed a small lever that was connected to the said crevice. The ball would shift across the top of the cube and unlock the door. The door was unlocked but not opened. The latch worked in the same way as the lever that came with my cube! By turning it I had opened nothing, but I had unlocked something. I excitedly turned to Andrea and explained my revelation.

"We've got to go back," Andrea whispered across the table.

"I know. We have to get back there tonight."

"It might be best to give it a night. The security will be tighter than ever. There is no way we will be able to breach it like we did last night."

"At least not in the same way. There is a way to cheat every system; you just have to think."

"Well, what are you thinking?"

"I have a little plan that might work."

We rapidly constructed our scheme. If only we could get to that tomb, it had to lead to something. There was a mystery waiting behind those walls, and I felt that I had to find my way into its hidden possibilities.

We went to dinner with Ben that night, our plan restlessly racing through our minds in imaginative rehearsal.

Partway through dinner, something terrible seemed to happen, something that appeared as though it would severely damage our strategy and delay our adventure; but in reality it was only part of our plan. Andrea rushed to the bathroom and pretended to vomit. Ben guessed it was something in the food. She came back and looked pale as ever.

We had only eaten our appetizer to that point, so Ben and I decided we would stay and finish our meal. But while we waited, I told him I would take Andrea out to the front of the restaurant and grab her a cab to take back to the hotel. While in front of the hotel, we snuck Andrea into the back of Ben's van. I had been sure to leave the passenger side door unlocked, therefore allowing access to the inside of his vehicle.

I returned to the dinner table to find our meals had arrived.

"Looks good." I smiled.

Ben's face remained straight for a minute before he finally looked up, and slowly the crevice of a smile broke across his face. "How is the study going?"

"Uh, you know," I hesitated. "It's going all right. I mean, I'm learning."

Ben just stared into my eyes, his dark glare scanning my thoughts. "Well, I hope you find what you're looking for."

And that was it. That was all anybody said the entire meal. We ate in a heavy silence that seemed to come alive, breathing down our backs, stretching the seconds into minutes. The dinner lasted a half hour, but it felt like a lifetime.

Afterward, Ben drove me to my hotel. I worked my way up the two flights of stairs and prepared to carry out the plan.

At about ten thirty or so that night, Ben's familiar van pulled up to the front of my hotel, but of course, it was not the familiar driver. Andrea sat in the driver's seat with a smile, perched on her pride. I rushed over and took the wheel as Andrea scooted to the passenger side.

"Nicely done. Where is Ben?"

Andrea just turned to the back, and there Ben lay across the backseat, bound by tape. I laughed but shared a concerned thought with Andrea.

"There better be something behind that wall."

"If not, we are in big trouble."

"If *yes*, we are in big trouble. Just maybe the headlines will make us out to be heroes."

We both laughed, but the concern, no doubt, was real. Still, I crowned myself with Ben's raggedy, old, Red Sox hat and headed for the Zion gate. At the sight of Ben's van, the gates easily opened and allowed for our passage. I looked straight on and gave a quick wave to the guards then found some open space to park. Quickly, Andrea and I seized the opportunity to remain concealed. I tossed Ben's hat to the back of the van, and we raced into the tomb.

Desperately, we searched for the possible location of the door. We held onto a frail hope that it somehow had remained unlocked. I reached back behind the tomb to find the latch—it had been cemented over.

The search for the door continued in the hands of an urgent prayer. Then, as if it were destiny, Andrea spotted a crack. We seized the chance for truth, never letting go of our faith in possibility. Andrea and I worked our fingers into the cracks and pulled. The wall began to shift, and soon we had worked a hole big enough to allow for our passing.

Quickly we slipped through the opening and found ourselves in a dark, damp cavern. I switched on a flashlight, which chased the darkness into the depths of what looked like a deep tunnel. With nothing but ignorance, we shrugged and began the next leg of our journey. Step by step we crept into the darkness, hope promising answers to the mystery of what lay beyond the borders of my flashlight's rays.

We stared down the dark barrel of the greatest mystery in archaeological history. The sides of the walls were moist but smooth, and a jumble of mixed rocks formed the pathway.

"This is unbelievable," Andrea commented, her eyes dancing in amazement through the darkness.

"I know. This is absolutely incredible." Then, as we looked down at the gravel pathway, we noticed that the strange colors of the rocks seemed to create a special pattern.

"Hold on!" Andrea excitedly jumped at realization, her joy echoing down the tunnel.

I raced back up the tunnel to see where the pattern began. At this point we were near two hundred fifty yards into the mystifying, hidden lair of David's tomb, and we feared that soon someone would discover our great scheme.

I eventually got near the entrance when I looked down and saw the first series of colored stones.

"What does it say?" Andrea let the tunnel carry her whisper.

"I'm not sure, but it's not in Hebrew. It looks like it is Latin." I had studied Latin for four semesters in college and tried to reach back in my memory to decode this hidden message. As I began to translate, I suddenly realized what it was. It was the song of David, found in Second Samuel. "It is David's song of praise to YHWH, from the Old Testament."

"What does it say?"

"Well, it's actually only the first verse over and over again. 'The Lord is my Rock, my fortress, my deliverer/ my God is the rock in whom I take refuge/my shield and the horn of my salvation.'"

"So?"

"I'm not sure. This passageway must lead to some secret hiding place that David, or someone in Israel, had. He calls God his rock, and the words are decorated across a pattern of rocks. It seems to be a clue or a map or a guide or something. This was David's shelter or someone's shelter—when Jerusalem was seized, they sought refuge in here."

We continued on our journey into a dark abyss of mystery. The air got chilly as the tunnel began to twist and turn when we were about eight hundred yards in. We placed each step delicately in front of the other, ignorantly voyaging into the depths of an unknown world, clinging to the same hope that had carried us by the thin string of a desperate prayer into that very tunnel. Still, the greatest discoveries remained covered and in front of us.

We had been walking for about an hour when our next question challenged us to make a decision. There was a fork in the tunnel. We shone the flashlights down each, but not even light could guide us to an answer. I studied the entrances and even tried to walk down each, but it didn't work like that. The future was masked in uncertainty.

However, just beneath the ceiling of the right entrance was an inscription of a word in what looked like Aramaic. Aramaic was the language of Jesus and the apostles and disciples of the New Testament and also parts of the ancient Hebrew bible.

"What does this say?" I asked Andrea.

"*Kephas*."

That was it! *Kephas*, or *peter*, means *rock* in Aramaic! It was the name Jesus gave Simon in Matthew 16.

"This is the way we need to go."

"What makes you so sure? What does this mean?"

I explained the meaning of the name. Simon Peter was to be the rock upon whom Jesus would build his church. Filled with faith and confidence, we marched into the passageway. But not eighty steps into the new tunnel, something seemingly tragic happened. The ground came out from under us. We fell and crashed into a great pit.

It seemed like destiny; just when our faith in our journey felt at its highest point, the world was tragically ripped from beneath our feet. We stumbled, fell, and crashed, and so too did our confidence, our hope.

"Andrea, are you okay?" I pleaded into the darkness. Our flashlight went out upon impact with the ground. The darkness swallowed us in a gulp of mystery.

"Yes, are you?" All I could hear was her voice. I was blind, feeling my way across the bottom of the pit.

"Yes. Can you walk to my voice?"

"I can try." We both crawled across the floor, feeling in front of us, hoping to anticipate what would happen next but bracing ourselves for surprise.

"Ouch!" Andrea's voice echoed around the walls of our prison and disappeared in the darkness as it raced against the walls of the cavern.

"What happened?" I desperately asked, unknowing.

"I'm fine; there is just a rock here. It is huge. It says something on it. I can feel it. It is almost like brail, but the bumps make real words."

"Can you read it?"

"I'm trying." The silence signaled that she was reading it. "It says *Isaiah*!"

"Oh my God," I said, smiling. Isaiah was a prophet in the eighth century B.C.E. He preached about the inviolability of the temple. The temple was the place where God could be found, and when Jerusalem was attacked by the Assyrians in 701 B.C.E., the temple was the one place where they could seek refuge. We both knew. "Hold on, keep talking. I'm coming."

I found my way to her and felt the rock.

"Does it say anything else?"

"Yes. It says *Peter* again."

"We've got to move this rock."

We both began to push the rock, offering all our strength to shift the massive boulder. Simultaneously we heard approaching footsteps.

"Come on!" I whispered desperately into the darkness.

The footsteps grew louder and louder as they approached.

"Come on!" We both pulled and pushed, and all the while *boom*, *boom*, against the rocky pathway above.

Then, slowly, it began to shift. Beneath was what felt like yet another dark tunnel, but this one seemed more like a slide. *One more leap of faith*, I figured.

"Let's go." I decided, and then, with only the slightest hesitation, I plunged into the unknown, armed with this illogical faith in some mystery that lay beyond the darkness. Andrea jumped in behind me, and we slid against the walls of the slide, the footsteps fading, lost in the former abyss as we moved into a new one. The slide picked up speed as we raced at rapid speeds into the unknown. Eventually the tunnel spit us out, and what we saw when we opened our eyes would change our world forever.

Unlike the darkness from before, we now found ourselves in a new room of light. Gold blanketed the walls and brilliantly reflected some great shining figure in the center of the room. It was absolutely beautiful. Everything blended together perfectly; the light and gold and ceilings acted in perfect and harmonious continuity. Easily the light reflected the gold, and the gold reflected the light.

"Where are we?" Andrea whispered in amazement.

But it was a rhetorical question; we both knew. This was a hidden temple. They had built a temple above the ground, but that was not the real throne of God. This was where Isaiah and all of the Judeans came during the siege of 701 B.C.; this was where God's glory was truly witnessed. This was the foundation of their church, their religion, their life.

But more than that, this was a symbol. This was the one place in the man-ruled world where absolute beauty could be found. Hidden in the depths of darkness, lost in the abyss of mystery, cloaked in a hopeless cavern, it could only be found with the light of faith.

At that moment, we stood at the center of untainted purity, unobstructed harmony, and untouched beauty. It was a reflection of the world that YHWH had created, not the one that man had turned it into. It was honest justice and relentless mercy. It was ruthless compassion and illogical love. It was beauty beyond words.

Without reason I began to cry. I fell to my knees, and when I looked up I saw the most amazing thing yet. I saw this great light exalting beams of an unknown wonder, and then, through that, I saw a mysterious face. It came, and in a second it was gone. To this day, I swear it was the face of an angel or maybe the face of my parents.

This journey had turned into the greatest spiritual adventure of my life. My faith was revived, my hope renewed. I felt the light fill my body and my life. I turned to Andrea, and we embraced in a moment of perfect bliss.

"Beautiful, isn't it?" Ben's voice boomed from the darkness. Both Andrea and I were stunned.

"Ben—"

"No," he interrupted. "It's okay. This is, as I'm sure you've deciphered, the temple of YHWH. It was built by Solomon in secrecy, with additions from each generation after him, passing the secret down the line of David's descendants. Only a limited number of people learn in their lifetime, and they are sworn to secrecy and to protect the secret at all costs."

"But why a secret?" Andrea asked for both of us.

"Because it has to be. If this becomes a tourist site, then the point of it will be diminished. One of two things will happen, should the world learn of this. Either they will disregard the faith that accompanies its beauty and just gaze, take pictures, etc., or the entire world will come to believe and see its truth."

"What is wrong with the second one?"

"First of all, it isn't worth the risk of the first. Secondly, the world must learn to believe by faith. You, you endured a test of faith and have now seen the wonder of God. The world, they will just see. There is no faith, no failure, no trouble. They would never trip and fall, never rely on hope. The answer will simply be cast in front of them— and afterwards their lives will go on. Life…well, life is not meant to be an image of justice. Life is spontaneous, random, and the only order exists in God and what we allow God to create between us. At any moment we could die. It may not seem fair, but that is not the point. Life is not unfair, but it is not fair—it is life. We just have to have faith that somehow there will be resolve. We must have hope and persevere. People must let God absorb their life and trust in the mystery of possibility."

Andrea and I stood in awe. This man we had taken as a jerk was in fact a keeper of the greatest secret in the world. And now we were too.

With Ben's help, we found our way back out of the cavern. We finished our study over the last few days of our stay. Ben recommended me for a big project in South America, and Andrea and I returned home with the hope of possible future success.

My faith had been burnt by the fire of skepticism. My hope of a greater reality had crumbled beneath the incongruities of the one I lived in. I walked faithless, lightless, through a dark world. And now, in an unexpected turn, light erupted from the walls of my world. Nothing *really* changed around me—I was able to write a few insignificant reports, detailing the unimportant excavations I *officially* completed, but I still lacked any major status or respect as an archaeologist. My greatest discovery would go unseen and fostered a change only beneath my skin.

As we flew back across the ocean I looked out through the window of the plane. It was beautiful. It was peaceful, natural—one entity, in perfect harmonious continuity. The world as God had created it.

The Rocket Man

The stars stared down from heaven as I sat in an open field outside my house in Nebraska. A light breeze danced through the trees and ran its smooth fingers through my hair. I looked back up at the night sky and saw balls of gas burning billions of miles away, drizzled across the black universe like tiny freckles of light, small marks of hope keeping the night alive until the sun rose again. Sitting there, I felt at the heart of the galaxy. I wondered if the stars felt the same as they stared down at me.

The next morning I would be heading to Houston. I am an astronaut, and I was scheduled for liftoff in just two days—they had given me a few days at home before the expedition. I'd been training for years and dreaming for a lifetime. The anticipation was building in my stomach. My mind found peace as it soared through the stars, but my heart met some restless instability. I wondered how alone we really were. I imagined how little we really know. I felt the cold of the darkness press on my skin but still imagined the heat of those flaming lights that littered the blackness.

I had always dreamed of going to space, of sailing on the breath of angels through the hidden mystery beyond the borders of the world. I used to lie on my bed and imagine it lifting from my room and carrying me, and the entire world, by the fragile string of uncertainty and then simply drifting into the depths of the darkness. And now I lie as a grown man, the swift breeze kissing my skin with gentle lips, feeling the same restless hope but only days away from being cast into the darkness, only to become another ball of fire burning in the sky.

Eventually, I stood up and began the journey across my backyard and into my house. I went upstairs and saw my little girl sleeping in her bed. I kissed her forehead and said good night, returning to my empty cot, where I closed my eyes and let the darkness fill my dreams.

"Daddy, daddy, it's time to go!" My daughter jumped on the end of my bed and scurried to my side, pulling on my ears and whispering excitedly in my ear. "Daddy, it's time to go into outer space!"

I just smiled and pulled her tight, feeling her small body against my arms. My heart felt tired already as it prepared for the goodbye I would have to say. Grace was five years old. Her curly hair twisted from her head in waves of brown, and her beautiful eyes were a vaporous mix of colors, like supernovas of blue and green.

I crawled from bed, Grace clinging to my shoulders and gripping my heart. I reached over my head and swung her around my chest.

"Swoosh! Prepare for liftoff." I mimicked the sound of starting engines and tried to shake her body in imitation of the vibrations. She just giggled and closed her eyes, preparing for the journey, letting her imagination generate a world of possibility inside her heart.

We walked down to the kitchen, and I made eggs and pancakes, all while listening to Elton John singing "Rocket Man."

"Daddy, are you a rocket man?"

"Yes, Grace. Tomorrow I will be like Rocket Man."

"Does that mean I am Rocket Girl?"

I just smiled. "Do you want to be Rocket Girl?"

She nodded as she sipped her chocolate milk and swallowed a bite of blueberry pancake.

"Then you are Rocket Girl. And you know what, if it wasn't for you, I might be too scared to be Rocket Man."

The comment seemed to stop at my lips and miss her ears as my breath crumbled, the words drifting as a lost whisper. I worried about losing her; I worried about her losing me.

After breakfast, we headed for the airport and took off into the sky. The flight was about three hours, and I spent most of it staring out the window, watching the clouds pass by. We encountered some fog over Oklahoma, and I wondered how the pilot could see. I figured he had radar, but what made him trust the radar? I guessed some things you just trust to be honest, and you take them on faith.

Threads of Truth

Sometimes, in the face of uncertainty, we just have to trust what we have to tell us some truth.

The plane landed in Houston at noon, and Grace and I went and picked up our luggage. NASA provided a ride from the airport to the base, where we would spend the night and meet up with my sister, Brittany. Brittany was going to watch Grace while I was gone.

"Josh!" Someone called from across the airport. I turned to see an old friend, Ryan Smith, who worked at the NASA base, waving a hand in the air.

"Mr. Ryan!" Grace sprinted, arms open, toward Ryan, who kneeled to greet her with a hug. I approached slowly behind and extended a hand.

"How you doin,' Ryan?"

"The usual. Hanging in there." Ryan shot a smile and proceeded to grab one of the bags from my hand. "All right, we are parked in the back lot, so you can just follow me."

We trucked through the airport and found our way to the back parking lot, eventually coming to Ryan's 4-Runner. We threw the luggage in the trunk, Grace in the backseat, and headed down the highway toward the NASA base.

"You nervous?" Ryan broke a growing silence.

I turned and gave a quick grin. "A little bit. This isn't quite the same as the adventures we used to take, or pretend to take, as kids."

"Sure it is." Ryan laughed. "Only I won't be there, which means it won't be nearly as fun." He turned to me and gave a broad smile.

We pulled up to the base and unloaded everything onto a cart, working our way up to my room. Grace holding my hand, Ryan by my side, I caught a glimpse of the shuttle through my window. A shiver dribbled down my spine like a drop of cold water. I looked down at my watch: twenty hours until liftoff.

That night we ate at a restaurant attached to the base. I had a solid twelve-ounce steak, and Grace took down a good serving of mac and cheese. Afterward we went to our room, and I tucked Grace into her small bed. I picked her up and tickled her side, just to get a laugh, and wrapped the sheets around her warm body. It felt like the last time, for some reason. Some strange sensation consumed me as I pulled the covers up to her chin and padded the pillow beneath her head.

"Daddy, tell me a story."

"All right. But I warn you, I don't really know any good ones."

"It doesn't have to be true, Daddy."

"Yeah? All right, well. Um... I think I got one. Once upon a time, there was a man. He was a pretty normal guy. But he had really big dreams. You know what they were?" I paused. "He wanted to fly across the universe. He wanted to sail back into time. He wanted to see how it all began, to meet God, and see him make the world. He wanted to blast through the sky and rocket through history. He wanted to meet everyone who ever lived and hear their story. Nobody told him it was possible; they told him that life just didn't work like that. Well, you know what he did? He built himself a shuttle for his dreams, jumped in, hit the button, and off into history he flew. He saw it all, Grace. He met everyone and heard their story. He went past all the stars, and you know what he found at the heart of it all? It was this ball of fire, burning like a star, but even brighter and hotter. And this fire, it was made up of everything good in the world: love, faith, and hope. He dove into the ball to find God, to see where that true beginning was, and then it hit him. That ball of fire was God; God was love and hope and even faith itself. And from God, from love, the universe was made."

I looked down at my young daughter. Nothing I said made sense to her, but I imagine she just wanted to hear my voice. Slowly her eyes grew heavier like dense shutters, closing the window to her imagination. And off she went on the shuttle of her dreams, off to the heart of her own universe.

I walked over to my bed and crawled in. I looked out the window one last time, closed my eyes, and faded into a dream.

I woke up the next morning at eight o'clock and got breakfast before preparing for my flight. I got on my suit, kissed my sister good-bye, shook Ryan's hand with a smile, and embraced Grace for a final time. Then off I went to board the shuttle. I felt the television cameras on me as I and a crew of six others walked in a staggered formation down a tunnel toward the launch pad, taking in our final breaths of air before finding our way into the ship that would take us one, small, baby step into the great mystery that lies beyond the borders of our atmosphere.

We entered the crew cabin and found our places. Jim was the main pilot, and he assumed his position. I sat as the copilot; Lauren took a seat directly behind me, and Mike just behind Jim. Tyler, Taylor, and Ben sat beneath us on the lower deck of the shuttle. We got ourselves comfortable and conversed anxiously, yet with a burning excitement that might have alone been enough to blaze through the sky.

Main base ran some safety checks and prepared us for liftoff. After going through all the preliminary cautions, the countdown began. My heart throbbed beneath the cage of my chest. I felt the engines roar behind me. The shuttle began to vibrate and felt as though it shook violently. Five, four, three—I closed my eyes and took a quick gasp of air, trying to muster every bit of courage that remained un-deterred by anxiety. Two, one—and with a great explosion, I felt the shuttle lift into the air.

I imagined the people on the ground, watching the shuttle lift; I imagined Grace's eyes lighting up. I imagined a great cloud of smoke consuming the earth beneath as all the fire in hell surged from our engines. Up, up, up and into the abyss we coursed. Jim and I frantically checked all gauges to ensure a proper liftoff was in process. Finally, minutes later, we met peace as we leveled off into a great darkness. I felt like God, looking down at his creation. Then I turned to look out the other side and realized the multitude of darkness, the magnitude of the universe, the minuteness of our planet.

Eventually, we lifted our masks and undid our seatbelts to inhabit the airless chamber, only reminiscent of the ones created by NASA for training. For a few minutes we all just floated and swam through the nothingness and stared in awe at the world below.

"Beautiful, isn't it?" Jim smiled. He was a veteran, along with Taylor and Lauren.

I smiled back and searched for a response, but all I managed was a speechless nod and a weak cough as I choked on the air I tried to swallow.

"Just makes you think. How can the world be so chaotic, filled with such evil, corruption, war, and hate; but up here it is just a wondrous product of the universe."

"Just makes you think about God, huh?" I finally mustered from my lips.

"God?" Jim laughed. "Look around you. Space is God. The universe is God. Science is God."

"Well, I imagine the two can be reconciled."

"Reconciled?" Jim continued to snort. "Josh, come look at this." He pointed out the window. "You see that? That's South America. You know how many different religions there are there? You know how convinced each is that their god is the true God? Now look, on the other side of that ocean is Africa. Look at the United States; imagine the Middle East. See that little dot in the Pacific? That is Easter Island. Easter Island once had some ancient civilization. Ever wonder what they believed? Imagine all the people who have ever lived; now look around. People are just tiny specks of dust in a sandstorm. We search for significance; we make everything center around us. It is our natural tendency—but *look* around! We are the products of science, the result of physics. There is no reconciliation. There is science, there are the properties of physics, and from there came life. And now life thrives to find some importance, but really we are just the smallest parts of a massive, beautiful, solar system, galaxy, and entire cosmos. The only significance we have comes from the simple fact that we are alive."

I stared down at the planet and looked out at the stars. I searched my faith for an answer, but it gave none.

"Just think about it. Now let's get to work."

And so I returned to the shuttle and began to prepare for our project, of which pertained to making certain adjustments to a satellite. Meanwhile, the world continued beneath, in all its usual tendencies. I felt separated from it all. It was as if I were dead and just staring down, knowing that it continued to go round and that the sun continued to rise. I wondered what pressed time forward.

For dinner we ate interesting variations of normal food. Space food is specially processed to make it easily digestible, palatable, and made for consumption in an environment of zero gravity. Still, I swallowed it down, my stomach embracing every nutrient that served to fill it.

The atmosphere was light and fun; Taylor and Tyler joked as Lauren, Ben, and Mike laughed along. Mike brought a harmonica, which he used to serenade the crew with small medleys. All felt natural; all felt at peace, happy.

Later that night I held a picture of Grace and stared out the window at the cavernous emptiness that lay cast in a sea of darkness. There was no horizon, no sky, no ground, just a distant continuum of space. My eyes chased the dark for the flickers of lost stars.

Jim again came up and sat next to me.

"Hey, Jim. How's it going?"

"Not too bad, Josh. What are you thinking about?"

I turned and smiled at him. "You ever wish you could just cast off and drift into space? Just let the emptiness carry you to some far-flung star or hidden planet; just sift softly into the discovery of a whole new universe?"

Jim laughed. "Well..." He paused. "Well, yeah, I guess that would be pretty cool."

"Why don't you believe in God, Jim?"

"How could I?" Jim turned to the far side of the shuttle, where the image of the world remained trapped by the borders of a windowsill. "How could I believe in a God who was willing to create men who were eternally damned, condemned for simple ignorance? I can't bring myself to believe that those who pick the 'wrong God' or are just never exposed to the 'right' one are just destined for hell. The way I see it, the presence of science gave the world structure, and the absence of God allowed for the chaos and inconsistency that exists within that life."

I just stared out the window and imagined all those souls who remained lost without salvation, sprinkled through history like cursed spirits, only to be found by the fires of condemnation. My stomach turned. How had I been so lucky? How had I been so blessed? Had I been chosen for heaven by birth? Did God just have some list, and those who weren't on it were only meant to struggle on the streets or some third-world country, a virtual hell, searching for the peace of death only to have their one hope at serenity damned by fate? To my left, I saw a wave of fireballs dance across the darkness, shooting like a fading hope into some uncertain abyss.

"You know, my life has been perfect. I have no reason to doubt anything. Great parents, great friends, great dreams, great opportunities; but how could one not be skeptical? Look around you. Why would some benevolent God have created a world with such evil potential?"

Again I stared out the window, searching for a sign, anything, to affirm my faith. I prayed to feel the soft Nebraska breeze tussle my hair, but my faith crumbled in my doubtful fist. I wanted to feel the assurance I had felt then. I wanted to shed the cold skin of my doubts.

"I'm not saying this world is any less miraculous. Indescribable sensations surround us every day, but they are only products of some incredible universal story. We are products of the universe, which is a product of itself. We die and turn to dust, which becomes the dirt, which fosters the grass, which gives life to life in some eternal cycle. It is so beautiful. It is faultless. You're looking for a perfect God to believe in? Believe in that—the world around you, the grass you walk on, the stars in the sky, the sun to rise in the morning. That is the one true consistency we have to depend on."

"B-but?" I stuttered. I looked down at the picture of Grace. I gaped out the window, pleading the stars for answers.

"Good night."

Jim left and went to strap himself in for sleep. I followed shortly behind him.

Threads of Truth

I imagined Grace down on Earth. I imagined that she gazed at the stars before her eyes found our shuttle, a quiet flame coasting through the darkness. I imagined she said a prayer and whispered it to the wind, allowing it to carry her words to my aching ears. I listened and let them talk me to sleep.

I woke up to chaos. Jim was shouting at the crew to wake up, and I quickly prepared myself for emergency. Jim approached me in a controlled panic, his eyes burning yet his voice steady.

"NASA believes there is something wrong with our shuttle. They think something might have happened during liftoff. Some debris might have hit one of the orbiter wings or fuel tanks. We have to reenter, but even that has its great risks. Still, we don't really have a choice. Tyler is preparing to go out there to take a look."

"Tyler? Who is going with him? I'll go." I quickly got myself assembled and organized for exit from the shuttle.

I hung from the side of the shuttle, harnessed back to the ship by a chord as Tyler went beneath the orbiter to inspect for damage. He found minor damage possible to the rear body flap and possibly the TPS—which would be more severe; and with that we returned bearing the disconcerting news. The TPS is the Thermal Protection System, which protects against the heat from the atmosphere upon reentry.

"Well, it is not as bad as it could be. We will probably be all right. Let's hope it is not the TPS. We have to reenter to be sure, though." Jim maintained communication with the NASA base, and both agreed on the course of action to cancel the mission and return home.

"All right, we must not be over alarmed. This is a minor situation, and I have full confidence that we will be okay. We must simply remain composed, follow procedure, and prepare for reentry."

We prepared the shuttle and returned to the crew cabin. Thankfully, after only a day we had maintained ample enough positioning to successfully land in Houston. It would require slightly more skilled maneuvering, but the task was by no means impossible. And so it began.

In my left chest pocket beneath my suit I carried the picture of Grace, and in my right, a picture of her mother, who had died just two years earlier in a house fire. My stomach churned, anxiety pulsing through my veins like a coursing river, threatening my sanity, yet still I forced my mind to retain some sense of posture.

Slowly we worked our way toward the planet, finding our way back into the atmosphere. I felt so far away but quickly imagined how little I had truly explored into the magnitude of our universe. The heat grew as we approached nearer the borders of our planet. My eyes remained glued to the reading from the TPS as Jim frantically navigated and communicated with NASA. Jim's eyes intensified with the heat, cutting through the sky, focusing, honing in on our destination, the guardian angel of all our lives.

The shuttle began to shake and vibrate, the heat growing more and more intense; we felt on the verge of catastrophe, at the mercy of destiny. And we continued our adventure of reentry. Slowly the body of the land unveiled itself behind a hazy cloud of smoke. Deeper and deeper, closer and closer we continued. And then it happened.

The TPS malfunctioned, and a great explosion filled the sky. The ship burst into a phantom of flames, a miasma of smoke, a fog of dissipating spirits. All in a second I felt my soul explode across the sky, stretching around the horizon, flooding the atmosphere in a blustery haze.

The greatest sight of all for me came just as the explosion filled my body with an unworldly heat. I saw great supernovas light up my face. And in them I saw Grace's face; I saw the face of her mother; I saw, even, the face of God himself. I felt inside my heart this sudden affirmation that had all along been hidden under questions of doubt. It was this internal, intrinsic, inherent faith. It was the same emotion that made me love Grace, that made me feel compassion for those lost souls, that made me feel hope for mine.

There was a natural spirituality draped across my heart, put in place so that I could believe—the only mark of evidence left by God alluding to his existence. It was a great surge of emotional confirmation, some type of inner radar. I wondered why I trusted it, but then again, I suppose, in the face of uncertainty, sometimes we just trust what we have to guide us to some truth. Beneath the heat of the atmosphere, I suddenly realized the significance of man beyond his breath. I felt, yet did not understand, the complexity of worldly reconciliation. I felt the stories of all those before me and inscribed my own in flaming letters across the backdrop of time.

And then, I took off into the universe, hand in hand with Jim, burning through the great abyss, launching ourselves through time to find the heart of the universe. By the fire we were consumed, through the fire we came, and for the fire of truth we searched. Ravaging through the darkness, grazing the stars, holding on to the certainty of possibility.

In the Darkness

Disbelief. Shock. Realization. Grief. Acceptance. These are the emotions we encounter when we learn of someone's death. The process varies in length depending on how well we knew them and how much we liked them. For some people, the emotions come and go like a flash of heat, a quick wince of surprise and sadness and then an easy acceptance. For some, the emotions are slow and articulate. They are obvious and clear, roughly working their way through the veins and stopping at the heart.

For me, when I learned of my father's death, I thought I would be like the first. His memory would quickly fade from my life and time would move on. I was right.

The last time I had seen my dad before his death was at a family reunion in Morocco, where he was born. I went mostly to see my mom, but his presence was unavoidable. We said our un-heartened hellos and shared a meek good-bye, then that was it. I hugged my mom and boarded a plane for New York.

I am a reporter for the *New York Times*, and I am good. I am really good. I have travelled the world, written leading stories, and supplied crushing headlines. My dad played no part in any of that. As far as I could tell when I was young, my father was a stubborn man, convinced of his beliefs, ignorant to possibility, and unaccepting of anything beyond the borders of his faith. I preferred open-mindedness.

The phone call came at one in the afternoon on a Monday. I was in my office, and the phone rang.

"Hello."

"Aaqib, it's Mom."

"Mom, my name is Adam now." Aaqib means *follower* in Arabic. While my father was a very religious Muslim, I changed my name when I came to America. My lack of faith in Islam created too much irony with the name.

"Your father has passed away."

"What?" Disbelief.

"Yes, he died early this morning."

"Wow." Shock.

"His procession will be this weekend. You must come."

The realization came, and quickest of all I felt a flash of grief pulse against my heart but then easily rebound and fade into indifference.

"Um. I'll have to see. I am writing a story—"

"Aaqib! He was your father. You will be here." My mom's quick tongue cut through the telephone line. There was no argument.

I hung up the phone and returned to my desk. The emotions had passed, and my day continued, but my journey to Morocco over the weekend would mark the beginning of a great adventure that would challenge my indifference and change my life.

My plane left at eight in the morning on Saturday. I woke up, and the warm June air of New York was dense and moist. Humidity from the nearby water stuck to each breath, and pollution surfed in the light breeze like some unavoidable stench, torturing the senses and blackening the lungs. After twelve years living in the city, it smelled like home.

The plane was big, fit with three rows of seats and two walking aisles. I sat in coach in a far right window seat, next to a heavyset man in his mid-forties. He had a fear of flying, and an anxious sweat burned through his undershirt and began to show beneath his arms and around his neck. For most of the flight I just stared through the window and watched the clouds wisp past like faceless ghosts.

I was relatively mute for the entire trip. It wasn't that I was depressed so much as I was reflecting. I tried to be sad. I tried to recall some happy moment, just one joyful memory, one day, hour, or minute cloaked in laughter that my father and I had shared, but I came up empty.

We experienced turbulence when we passed over England and approached our initial destination of Frankfurt, Germany.

I reflected not so much on my dad but on life itself. If there is one thing death does, be it someone you know or don't know, like or dislike, it makes you realize the fragility of life. What if that plane had crashed? What if I had a heart attack? What if the guy sitting next to me was a madman and decided to shove a giant peanut down my throat and choke me? It sounds humorous, and death may always seem so far away, but it isn't. It is this invisible spirit tracing our every footstep, waiting for us to slip, waiting for the opportunity to intercept our lives and bring us to his dimension of existence.

The thought gave me shivers. I boarded the next plane for Morocco and encountered the same thoughts for another couple hours. I tried to be sad again and tried to write something about my dad for the funeral.

I was expected to speak.

When I got off the plane and entered the Anfa airport in Morocco, my mom stood there waiting for me. I gave her a warm hug, understanding her struggle, and tried to absorb her pain through our embrace.

"I'm glad you are here, Aaqib."

"Mom, it's not Aaqib—." Her face looked so empty. "I'm here, Mom. I'm here."

She drove us about a half hour back to her house just outside of Casablanca. Lots of family—my grown-up cousins, my mom's siblings, and my dad's only surviving brother—occupied the house, which was thick with sadness. Dried tears stuck to everyone's faces.

I felt guilty for not feeling sad; I really did. He was my father, he raised me, and I felt nothing but those initial emotions.

I showed myself to the room I usually stayed in and placed my bags near the bedside. The walls of the room were decorated with pictures of me and pictures of my father, but only one of us together.

The picture was from our trip to Mecca, our *hajj*. In the picture, my dad is smiling. He looks so proud, so at peace. I am not. I remember the day too. I remember not wanting to be there, not believing in anything we saw, and thinking my dad foolish for believing in any of it. My dad tried to force-feed me the religion, and I resented him for that. If nothing else, he wanted me to accept his religion, to be like him, and he never considered what I was feeling. He ruined our relationship. My mom had forced me to be in the picture. Looking back, I regret not smiling.

That night we ate dinner and the mood lightened. Family shared funny stories and memories from childhood and of my dad. People laughed, and it was as if my dad had come back to life to join us at the dinner table. Not in a literal sense, existing in an exact moment of time, but through a random selection of connected memories, this image of my dad through his life—past, the once present, and the ended future—seemed to be created. Not a man in one second of time, but a boy, a child, and a man all present simultaneously through the power of memory.

After dinner I returned to my room and prepared to go to sleep. I stared blankly at the walls, trying to dream up some speech for the next morning, but my eyes were heavy from jet lag, and I quickly surrendered to sleep.

The next morning, fittingly, clouds were cast across the skies, leaving the earth beneath lost within an ominous, gray shadow. The viewing was to be at ten that morning.

I stumbled down the stairs and met my mother for breakfast in the kitchen. She made eggs, cooked sunny side up, and toast. We ate in silence as my mind still searched for words to say later that morning. Still, even deep contemplation next to the woman who loved him most left my thoughts arid and dry, nothing with the emotional value expected. I realized that was what I was scared of more than anything—not meeting expectations. Not fulfilling my role sufficiently. I made myself sick; this was just another job.

Ten o'clock came, and there the casket sat. Opened and readily prepared to be seen. I approached the unclosed tomb with uneasy footsteps and peered in. I had never really seen a dead man before, never having been to a funeral. I had actually been to one, but it was my grandfather's after he had died in a fire, and he had a closed casket to mask his body's desolation.

It is a strange thing to see a dead body. It is just there. There are the eyes, the nose, the hair, the arms, the legs—everything perfectly attached and put together, but still there is something missing. There is no movement behind their closed eyes, an emptiness to their appearance. It is not as if they are sleeping, nor even just without the slow breeze of breath pumping an ebbing stomach, but rather it appears as though some other factor is missing. There is some other wind of energy absent from their presence. As obvious as it sounds, their body is there, their heart may be there, their organs may be there, but any trace of life has ascended or dissipated from the body. If I didn't know better, I'd say it was his spirit that was missing, but that is a little too cliché for me.

Threads of Truth

These observations raced through my mind as I stared down at my deceased father. I searched my face for a tear, but there were none. Then, forty viewers, an obituary, and a song later, I took the stand.

I stared down at my father's casket and prepared to speak. My heart pounded in my chest, and my mind raced. I was honest. I told of how my dad and I were never as close as a father and son should be. I said that I never really loved him but that I also never really knew him. To my surprise, the honesty evoked a tear from my heart. And then I finished my speech with a mention of how any time a life ends and a story closes, it is a call for mourning but also a call for celebration, and that I hoped we could all embrace for a little of both.

It went as well as I could have asked for, and the morning rolled on.

My plane was set to leave that evening at six so that I could have the day to spend with my mom and other family members. My dad's will was to be read at noon that day, but until that reading, I went for a walk with my mother.

The air was so thick and hot, the sun's fiery rays reached down from the sky to kiss my skin with flaming lips. She lived next to the shore, and we walked along the sandy beach.

"You know he loved you." My mom broke through the silence.

"Yeah. I guess so."

"What do you mean you guess so?" My mom's North African accent was sharp and articulate.

"We just never developed any type of relationship. We were too different."

"No. You were not very different. Too much alike."

"I was not like dad. He was stubborn and closed-minded."

"Oh, but you are very stubborn. And he might surprise you. He lived an entire life, you know. Not just the parts that you saw."

"Well, it's too late now, anyway."

"Too late for what? Too late to talk to him to his face? Yes. To hear his story? To know his story? It is never too late. A man's life is scripted through time, Aaqib. It is not a secret buried in a man's chest. It is written across the hearts of those he knew."

"So what, you expect me to just go on some mission to interview everyone he knew or met or was friends with and put together some story of my dad in my head? That's crazy."

"I don't expect you to, no."

"What does that mean?" I laughed and shot her a smile. She just shrugged, and I pulled her close to me for a quick hug. We continued down the beach, the soothing Atlantic pulsing against the shore in a continuing recycling of water. Each wave was new but made of the same waters as the last.

A lawyer read my dad's will. He was tall and lanky, dark skinned. He came to read the will at our house, dressed in a long, black suit with a bright red tie. He had the most indifferent look on his face, as if it wasn't a man that had just died but rather a mass of possessions had been liberated and none of it was for him. He was just there to read out the names of the new owner.

He sat down and briefly introduced himself as Sahjel Patuhl. My mother, several cousins, my father's last remaining siblings, and myself gathered around a table and prepared for the reading of my father's final wishes.

The house and other major possessions were left naturally to my mom. His books were left to my younger cousin Rajim, who loved to read, and his childhood belongings went to his brother. I didn't expect to be left with anything. I didn't even expect a good-bye. In fact, I almost hoped for nothing.

As things went, asset after asset was passed around the table. There was no joy in it for those who loved him, but at least, it seemed, they were obtaining some concrete memory beyond what the heart retains.

The lawyer came to the end of the list, and as fate would have it, one thing remained. A letter, addressed to me. The lawyer pushed the closed envelope across the table and closed his briefcase. My mother smiled, and everyone left the table.

I stared down at the letter and dreamed up what it might possibly say. I remembered so many things he had told me when I was growing up. I thought, surely this was some final stubborn effort to thrust his ideals into my life.

Read your Koran. Worship Allah. Challenge yourself. Don't do that. Follow your faith. Pray. Pray. I expected the type of things that sound like good fatherly quotes from a strong Muslim dad but are only remnants of a cold relationship. When something is forced into your life, like a harsh needle piercing your unsuspecting skin, it is almost always rejected, thrown away by the mind to drift as a dark memory through the tide of time.

I opened it up, slowly sliding my finger beneath the seal and feeling the paper separate and unglue. I reached inside for the letter. My mom stood in the far doorway, pretending to be invisible. I didn't see her, but I could feel her anxious eyes follow my hand as it unfolded the paper.

> Aaqib,
>
> Son, if you are reading this then I have died. I have gone to meet our creator. I trust you already know many things I will say to you here. Read about the faith you were born into and find Allah in your life.

I stopped and chuckled.

> I also hope that there may be something here that you will not expect. Aaqib, you were my only son, and I didn't know you. We fought, we disagreed, and I forced myself unto you; still, you rejected me. We became distanced, and it was because of an effort to become close. This is my fault, and I apologize to you for that. The truth is, I was not born with what I believed; I found it. My faith was not written across my heart at birth but was in fact discovered along the road of my life.

I want you to know me, if only in death. Now, perhaps you will not know me by speaking to me but by undertaking the journey that I undertook. I want you to follow the trail I did in reaching my faith, not so that you too will come to believe what I did, but so that you will know who I was and how I became so. I have a single plane ticket in your room at the house. It is inside a book on the shelf. I trust you will know which one. There is only one, because some journeys were meant to be taken alone. Some journeys are meant for solitude, for in the entirety of our lives we are the only thing we truly have. Our own self is our most lasting partner, and others we make part of our lives along the way. At the first destination, your journey will begin. I cannot tell you any more, and I cannot make you go—but you must have faith, if not in God, simply in me, and if not in me, then in life; and I must have faith that you will do what is right for you.

Although it may have never seemed it, I love you.

Father

I picked up my head, and at first I felt angry. It must have been phony. Thirty years, and it is not until death that he makes an honest and genuine effort for a grounded relationship? *No*, I thought, n*o way*. I tore the letter in half and walked past my mother to my room. The house felt heavier than ever, bearing down on my shoulders.

My mom's shattered voice whispered through the air and found my swollen ears. Sorrow dripped from her lips with every breath, occasionally drifting through the air and filling the room, sticking to the walls, gripping the furniture.

"Please go, Aaqib. He really did love you."

I stared at the wall and felt the dense air press on my skin.

"He used to get angry when we would talk about you. He would get worked up, but it was a sad anger. He wanted you to see what he had felt in his life. It was anger from sadness and sadness from love. Emotions are funny; they can feel one way but mean something completely different. He loved you, and it wasn't until he lay on his deathbed that he truly understood how much. It took true pain, true fear, and true regret to realize, but he did. Please do this, not just for me, nor for your father, but because I do not want you to grow bitter and feel remorse when you grow old."

I slowly turned around and faced my mother's tear-filled eyes. I stood up straight and reached out to feel her desperate embrace.

I walked to the bookshelf and opened the Koran. The ticket was there.

I packed my bags and left the next morning at ten o'clock. Neither I nor my mother said anything over breakfast, but I could see the light of optimism fill the broken pieces of her heart. Hope restored loss, future and present cradled the past, and sunshine filled the sky outside.

I boarded the plane, and my mother sent me on my way. I was headed for Tabuk in Saudi Arabia, the city in which my father grew up.

The flight was relatively short, and my thoughts remained for the most part empty, simply inhaling the sights provided by the window.

I walked off the plane and into the airport at around noon or so. I looked around, not knowing who I was looking for. My eyes scavenged through the many faces, some equally lost in the chaos.

"Excuse me, are you Aaqib?" A voice approached from behind.

"Yes. Well, actually, you can call me Adam. I take it you are supposed to pick me up?"

"Yea, I'm Matthew. I was friends with your father when we were growing up."

"Not to seem like I'm drilling you, but why were you not at the funeral?"

"I couldn't make it. Amazingly, my wife has also just passed. Besides, I celebrate your dad's life every day. He may be dead, but he is still alive in me, and you too, I bet."

"With all due respect, I hope not."

The man just turned to me, his dark eyes scanning my thoughts. "That is a pretty heavy thing to say."

"Yeah." I laughed. "You didn't know him like I did."

"Ah, and you did not know him as I did." A smile creased across his face. I had nothing to say and simply kept my head down as we worked our way through the airport and found my luggage.

He led me out to his car, an old Honda Accord covered in dents and scratches. He laughed, looking at it as we approached.

"She still does the job!"

I sat in the passenger side as we started out into the city.

"What am I doing here?" I asked anxiously, my voice strained by confusion and even annoyance.

"Well, I suppose I am just going to show you around town. Show you where your dad grew up, tell you some memories."

"That's it?"

"That's it." He chuckled and turned on his left turn signal.

"You're not going to read me your Koran, take me to a mosque, tell me how greatly my dad influenced your muslim faith or how you found it together?"

"Nope. Actually I am going to take you to a church."

"What?"

"I'm Christian, Adam. I'm not Muslim."

I just stared through the window. The life of my father seemed further away than ever, lost in a cloud of time, hidden in a fog of history.

We pulled up to a small church after a short fifteen-minute drive. The walls were burned and beaten, the grass surrounding it dead and filled with patches of dirt and sand.

"Your father and I were both little Muslim boys. We both had Muslim fathers, and both of them were very respected figures in the faith. We prayed five times a day, we gave alms to the poor, we worshiped Allah in every aspect of our lives. But my father became radical. He tied his body to a bomb and blew himself and a dozen other people up. He put a gun in my hand just before, and I watched the explosion. I watched as this great light, this burst of fire consumed my dad's and several others' lives. I heard screams, I found myself lost in the center of chaos. I dropped the gun and ran into a building nearby. I cuddled into a ball and cried."

"Oh my God."

A heavy silence consumed the moment. The air between us twisted and bent with the remembrance of that tragic event. I looked up at the church and examined the burns that lined its walls. Then it hit me.

"This is where it happened, isn't it?"

"Yes, sir. Smart man, Adam. I could never see my faith the same again. It felt foreign, suddenly. It felt distant, and I rejected it. Your father tried to bring me back. He told me of Allah's love for us; he told me that it was still a faith of passion and compassion, a faith of love and trust. I couldn't believe him. I rejected it, but he never let me let go. The community began to become consumed by this radical extremism that rippled across the city. Everyone who remained rejected me and seized this 'call' to violence. All but your father, that is. He never stopped loving me, and he never let me go. I eventually came back to examine my faith, and I found my truth in Christianity. It was because of your father that I came back to it. Had he pushed me away as the others had, I would not be where I am. He saved my faith. He saved my life."

A tear dribbled from his sad eyes and seemed to evaporate into the thick air, absorbing the two of us. A tear of memory, a tear of pain, a tear of joy, expanding from the heart of one into the heart of another.

"I am going to leave, and you are going to stay here. Someone will come soon, I promise."

He got up and walked to his car. The engine started, and he drove off into the horizon, a tail of exhaust trailing him the whole way. I would never see him again.

As the late afternoon approached, the sun began to shift across the sky, slowly floating like a flurry of light across the deep blue universe. I imagined the world without the sun. What if we woke up one morning, and the sun refused to rise? What if we woke up one morning and death had captured light and darkness gripped our lives? What if the sun were like so many devastated people, losing hope, tired of falling, restlessly anxious for peace, and one morning decided to let the night reign over day? We would have no time; life would just be this empty continuous void, this endless, hopeless cycle of life and death.

Flowers would die, trees would suffocate, and pain would rule the world. People would kill, and hearts would be thrown to the dogs of vengeance. Would it really be that different?

It is incredible—the impact that a single star, among billions, can have. How a single ball of light, one mark of hope, one lasting and eternal effort to continuously rise in the morning, can change the whole world.

I stared at the burns on the side of the church. *Why?* Why would you kill yourself? Why would you kill others? Why persecute Christians? Why persecute Muslims? Why persecute non-believers, Buddhists, Africans? Are we really that different? To kill for a God, if there is a God, seemed pointless. He obviously made them too. He obviously touched them too—just maybe in a slightly different way.

"Aaqib?" A new voice called from behind me. I quickly turned, jolted from my thoughts.

"Yes," I replied, standing up and reaching out a hand. He returned the gesture.

"My name is Ashoka. I knew your father very well when we were younger. We knew each other through the Mosque. We actually travelled together and even went to Mecca together."

"Ah, I see. Very nice to meet you, Ashoka. So, what is your assignment as far as dealing with me?"

"I am going to take you to Mecca."

"Okay, here it comes. This is more like what I was expecting from my father."

"Oh, I am not Muslim, my friend. I am Buddhist." The man laughed, and his dark brown cheeks turned a cherry red, a dimple on his left cheek pressing into his face.

"Then why Mecca?"

"Please, get into the car, my friend. I have a story to tell you about your father and me. I will tell you as we drive."

I stepped into his car and fastened my seat belt as the engine coughed and wheezed before a loud roar signaled it was ready for takeoff. Out behind the church I saw the sun begin to sink. I hoped it would not be the last time I saw it.

At first we drove in silence. Heading down the highway, we faced a deep darkness that seemed to fall like the black shadow of the universe, descending beneath the dim lights of the stars. Like a soft, silk blanket, it covered the world we saw, but still I knew that somewhere the sun was just rising. It set in my world and rose in another.

"So what's your story?" I asked, breaking the growingly comfortable silence.

"Your father was an interesting man. He had a great passion for truth, for life, for faith itself. I was not quite the same but admired that and desired it. He had this peace of heart that I coveted. I always had doubts, though. I always felt some reserve. I had tried Christianity, but Jesus, a man and God in one, made no sense to me. It seemed shamelessly invented. I tried Judaism, Christianity without the Jesus part." He paused and chuckled at the irony of his last statement.

"So I decided it was time to try Islam, and that's when I met your father. I was twenty-three years old, and he was twenty-four. We met each other in Medina and were both on a journey toward Mecca: him to confirm his faith, me to find mine; it ended up going the other way around."

We came to an exit at the right, and Ashoka merged onto the ramp. The car puttered as exhaust kicked up behind us with the thrust of acceleration. I looked out through my window and looked up to the stars. I am not spiritual, but for whatever reason I expected to see something other than the sky. I expected to see the whole universe open up, but I then realized how much of a mystery it all was and always would be. I realized the uncertainty in which our world spun; I faced the loneliness that accompanied the great darkness we floated in, and I appreciated, perhaps for the first time, the magnitude of the space in which we resided. I imagined someone peering through the scope of a telescope on distant star, gazing at earth, wondering if they were all alone to face the universe.

"So as we hit the trail toward Mecca, your father befriended me. We talked a lot about what we believed. I told him my story, and he shared his. Being young and rebellious, I openly began to challenge his, what seemed to me, unfounded faith. I don't think he ever really knew how unstable his beliefs truly were. By the time we reached Mecca, he seemed to be doubting everything that he had once declared as truth. Needless to say, I felt guilty. I was just waiting for Allah to smite me from the sky or something, you know. I was pretty ignorant, and I felt terrible." We both kind of shared a quick laugh.

"Anyway, we got to Mecca, and suddenly I was entering the holy ground with the biggest doubter in the world when I thought I had been travelling with the greatest of believers. So we started meeting people and talking with some pretty strong Muslim guys. I mean, these guys were convinced, and well, I guess they didn't say what your father wanted to hear. They talked about the will of Allah, the evil of America, and the radicalism he had seen transform his hometown. For me, I was completely turned away. I guess I was just not getting the right gist from Islam. I still don't think I really understand it, but for your dad, he just seemed like he was losing hope. He seemed lost, for the first time. And let me tell you, it is scary being lost, especially when you are in a place in your life where you have never been.

"Suddenly darkness stares you in the eye and dares you to make a move. Hopelessness dares you to feel in front of you and take a step toward some invisible light of happiness. You feel alone, you feel desolate, you feel trapped by the abyss of loneliness that captures your soul and seems to steal your heart. It's awful, and I could see it all in your dad's fearful eyes. I left and continued my journey to truth, and I eventually found something that made sense to me in Buddhism. It just kind of clicked for me; it worked. I can feel it working in my life every day, and really, that is what faith should do. It should consume your life and fill every shadow of despair with a glimmer of confidence, a sparkle of hope, a flicker of optimism. Your father, though, well, the darkness, the shadow won out. He was lost, and this spiritual journey had some reverse effect."

We pulled off the highway into a roadside gas station.

"I need to get gas ... if you want to run to the restroom."

"Sure," I agreed. "Probably a good idea." I left and walked to the front of the station. The lights were dimmed, and it looked very suspicious. As I approached, I saw that it was actually going out of business. It was being shut down. I turned around to head back to the car; I supposed we would have to find another place to fill up. But as I turned, I saw Ashoka's car jet back off onto the highway. He faded into the night and became lost in the blackness that colored the horizon.

"Wait!" I chased hopelessly into the trail of exhaust that was left behind. It was no use; he was gone, and I was lost, trapped in the darkness.

Threads of Truth

The stars slowly, almost one by one, began to hide behind the increasingly overcast skies. I tracked down the side of the highway, contemplating the story that Ashoka had told. I was angry, that's for sure. The night was warm but windy, and I had been abandoned at some nowhere on the side of a highway that, for all I knew, led me only farther into an uncertain darkness. I had faith in something to come along and rescue me, but I wasn't sure what, and I didn't know what to expect.

I walked for about an hour but eventually grew restless and dropped on the side of the highway in hopeless anguish.

"Why?" I bellowed into the sky, expecting an answer from the few remaining stars scattered throughout the atmosphere or perhaps from the clouds that drifted on air through the darkness; I hoped for an answer from anything, possibly even my father. Possibly even God.

I remembered the plane trip over the ocean, the faceless ghosts that haunted my window. I remembered my father's spiritless body lying in its final resting place. I remembered my mother's hopeless eyes but her optimistic smile promising perseverance. I remembered the burns on the side of church. Why did those people die? Why were they willing to die for some God that they knew nothing about, except for what they read of their ancestor's history and, perhaps more importantly, because of what they felt?

Darkness can make one feel immensely despondent, but somehow it awakens a natural hope that seems carved across a man's heart, a powerful faith that clothes our spirits. I had never been spiritual before, but somewhere in that darkness I felt a part of me awaken. Somewhere in the midst of my most desolate state, I felt my heart awaken in a moment of hope, and life entered my body. I wondered if my living body had seemed as a walking version of my father's dead one, up until that moment. I caught hold of that feeling and swore to never let it go. It became a part of me, and I promised to never separate from it.

As I lay there, two headlights shone down the empty highway. They grew brighter and brighter, like the distant stars I peered at earlier, only burning through the light years of space between us, two meteors of hope destined to crash into my life.

The car pulled off the road about five yards to my left. The engine turned off, and out of the driver's side stepped a familiar being. It was my mother.

"Hello, Aaqib."

"Mom?" I stumbled over the word, almost in disbelief but too exhausted to be truly shocked.

"Yes, Aaqib. It is my turn to tell you my story of your father. When I met him, he was a spiritual wreck, that is for certain. His faith was in shambles and so too seemed his life. I couldn't help but feel compassion for him. I too had come from a Muslim family and prayed to find a way to help him. I met him in a coffee shop in New York. We got to talking, and in one of those incredible moments that we sometimes have with complete strangers, he told me his whole story. I knew nothing of what to say. I told him that I was Muslim and that I only prayed he could find his faith. We shared a moment of pure, beautiful, empathetic silence, and then something came to me.

I told him, 'Whenever I doubt my faith, I just read the Koran. I just read the Arabic; I inhale it, take it in and I feel the language. I feel the beauty of the words and let them work on my soul.'

"He stared at me like I was crazy. I walked out of that coffee shop feeling like a failure. Just a month later, there was a man knocking at my door. In his hand he held the Koran. He smiled and said nothing. We both knew what had happened. His faith had been renewed, fortified, and rediscovered. It had been challenged and rejected but finally reaccepted. He vowed he would never let go of that faith he found in his darkest moment. He swears it pulled him through it, and he promised to live by it."

I smiled back. "I completely understand."

We both stood up and walked to the car. My mother started the engine, and off into the distance we drove. Over the horizon, the sun—just as I had hoped and as it always did—began to rise. I had made the first leg of my journey, but the highway ahead of me was long. At least now I had the strength of hope, the promise of perseverance, and the light of faith in some truth to guide my way.

My father came across to me as too close-minded, trying to shove his faith down my throat at all costs— it turns out the cost was our relationship. I had always disrespected him, but only because I refused to hear his story. I rejected his beliefs as some memorized ideology and chose to remain ignorant to the tale that lay behind his faith. In just a single day I relived a microcosm of his journey, and empathy filled my heart. For the first real time, I cried for my father's death and for his life.

Patrick Piccolo

I had met a Christian and a Buddhist on the journey to understanding the faith of a Muslim. I decided to become a man of every religion. I decided to become a believer in the different manifestations of God. It was all the same being, I thought. It is all the same God, just put in different terms, so that all can relate and feel his glory.

For some, Christianity answers the spiritual questions we ask, for some it is Buddhism, and for some Islam, but for me it was different. Faith was a collective history of the religious experience, and I simply came to believe in the one God I felt ruled over all of these different ideologies. The God I found knows no name—he is simply God. I came to have faith in this God, in stories, and, most importantly of all, I came to have faith in hope. I came to believe that with each fall of darkness there would be the rising of the sun in the morning.

Just keep your eyes on the horizon, grip whatever fills your faith with peace and compassion, and don't let go until the light of hope approaches from the edge of the highway.

Those Last Few Moments

It was a Friday evening during the Pennsylvania summer. Young kids ended their wiffle ball games, teenagers prepared for the weekend, and adults celebrated the end to a long week of work.

The sky was calm and serene as the sun melted into shades of orange above the horizon and stretched its bloody fingers across the earth's ceiling in a final breath of light. The scene was perfect. A simple summer day, come and gone like so many before it, only to repeat itself with the blink of an eye.

That is all the night really is—a blink of time come and gone like a dream.

Just beneath this beautiful sunset lay ol' Brian McNamy. He was seventy-three years old. His skin was wrinkled, his eyes were blurred, his bones were brittle, and his heart was beaten by bruised loves and crippling attacks. Still, his spirit and his mind carried the memories, the energy, and the passion that had come to define his life.

His room was dark as family mourned his illness and saw life fade from his eyes as time stole every last, precious breath from his chest. Cries rattled the dense air as tears filled the broken ridges of his loved ones' hearts. His heart pulsed at an inconsistent tempo as preachers prayed and doctors restlessly closed their medicine books—the end was as near as the night.

This was the house in which he was born nearly a century before. The room across the hall gave birth to his first dreams, his first hopes, his first successes and failures, and now, a lifetime later, after he'd seen all those dreams thrive and die, he found himself a hallway away from where he had started.

The noise in the room grew as the pain in his chest throbbed. Outside, the peace remained untouched—and then he blinked. Behind his eyelids the darkness faded into an explosion of light. The mournful screams dimmed into silence. He felt his spirit sprint through the corridor of time that was his life—this is what he saw.

I was born July 5, 1918. I don't exactly remember the day, but it is one of those things you are told stories of so many times, it seems to be engraved in your memory.

I'm told I had blond hair at birth, but within eight weeks it had turned a light brown, with only flashes of blond twisted around my curls. I'm told I was a happy baby, which makes me wish I remembered those days with more distinction, but I suppose I still lived them through the memories and stories of my parents and uncles.

My memory truly starts at about the age of five. I can still clearly see my fifth birthday. I remember my mom's home-baked cake, a memory in itself from her Irish heritage, baked with graham cracker, glazed in a thin slate of vanilla icing, topped with five candles, all lit and waiting to carry the weight of my wishes. At that point in time, however, my wishes weren't too heavy a burden to bear.

I had two sisters, both older. Mary was eight at that time, and Sara was twelve. My mom was a hard-working Irish mother, and my father a product of two Irish immigrants from the 1870s. My dad himself was born in the slums of New York during the late Industrial Revolution of the nineteenth century. He moved to a small town in western Pennsylvania when his dad lost his job after attempting to form a labor union at his workshop in New York. He came to western Pennsylvania to join the mining business. My dad followed his footsteps, and, looking back, I had the same dark fate clouding my future, although it wasn't until years later that I would realize this destiny.

As a kid, I was a dreamer, especially compared to my peers. I never bought into the destiny that seemed inscribed across the billboard of my life. For that, the greatest piece of my history I have to thank is a game I didn't fall in love with until the age of seven—and that game was baseball.

Until my seventh birthday, my summer days consisted of shooting my Daisy BB gun at birds and squirrels down by the local cemetery. I would find a few pals from around town, and we'd all take off to the wooded graveyard, which became the birthplace of my imagination.

I would watch the sun set, and once it dipped behind the tree line, I would take off up a dirt path behind the cemetery, sneak under a chain-link fence, and dash through my neighbors' yards, dodging laundry lines and angry screams from those who caught me "trespassing" on their five-hundred-foot lots.

I would find my way home just in time to wash my hands and face before my dad got back from work. I would wait on the front doorstep to hear the restless engine of my father's old Ford, which seemed to cough up smoke all the way down the rocky street on which we lived. I used to admire his callused hands, stained a smoky black from an afternoon in the mines. To the world he was a simple, poor miner in western Pennsylvania; but to me, he might as well have been Hercules. I would rub tar on my face and stare in the mirror, trying to get my muscles to flex in the same way his tensed as he removed his shirt for a bath. Although today I see he may have been no superhero, there is no fooling my memories—he was my idol.

There is one day in particular that sticks out to me about my dad, though. One day I will never forget, out of the thousands of moments I spent with him that are glued so powerfully to my heart.

When I was seven, my dad took me on a day trip to Pittsburgh to watch the Pirates play the Cardinals. The drive was a good few hours that may have seemed like an eternity to a seven-year-old, but I wouldn't trade those hours for anything.

I remember pulling into the city and seeing giant smokestacks darkening the horizon. I remember my dad describing how it all worked and telling me the history of the city—a long list of random facts I have completely forgotten. But I will never forget the smile on his face as he shared every detail he could drain from his mind.

But more than anything, I remember seeing the baseball stadium for the first time. The moist air painted the grass in a thin layer of mist. The dirt looked so soft and smooth, like a blanket of brown silk carpeted across the infield. It was a heaven unlike any I had ever dreamed of, but from that point on it became the obsession of my sleep. Between those two white lines and ivy-covered wall I thought I saw paradise; all that was missing was God and his throne.

The Pirates lost that day—six to five in eleven innings. The Cardinals scored two in the ninth to tie it, and then Rogers Hornsby hit a homerun in the top of the eleventh to claim the lead and cap off the scoring for the night. The whole ride home I rattled on about the game and how one day that would be me. I turned to my dad and with all the confidence and faith in the world pronounced that one day I would step on that field, that one day I would play professional baseball for the Pittsburgh Pirates. My dad's eyes met mine, and he too reassured my faith.

My adolescence became centered around the game. I memorized the statistics of Babe Ruth, Lou Gehrig, and all of Murderer's Row for the Yankees. I would study the newspaper every morning—my ambition was fed by a growing passion and understanding for the game. I stopped shooting BB guns, and swimming in the

Allegheny took a back seat. I had a dream, and it gave me the wings of faith. It gave me the belief that the impossible did not exist. At that time, professional baseball did not seem so out of reach, but to me, more than anyone, it seemed as though it were my future, dangling in front of my face, begging for me to take hold.

I never did play baseball for the Pirates. In fact, I never did even step on that field, but believing in that dream gave me certain intangibles I could never trade. It gave me more gifts than it took away, and those gifts turned into a success of a different form as I traveled through the journey of my life.

A quick gasp, and Mr. McNamy was again jolted back to the present time. The doctors rose to their feet as even the walls seemed to cling to his breath. A prayer, a hope, swallowed abruptly into the chest of the old man. Another thrust of life into his heart.

Just as quickly, however, ol' McNamy felt his mind snatched from consciousness and dragged back through time by his memories.

I continued to dream, and those dreams continued to nurture my hope. However, just four years after that beautiful day at the ballpark, my dreams were interrupted, although that same hope would help me and my family to persevere.

The Great Depression was the scariest time of my life, although it didn't really hit us out in western Pennsylvania until a few months into it. I was eleven years old at the start of 1930 and lived with the same innocence that characterizes every little kid. As if nothing had happened, I made my usual route one morning down to the cemetery with a group of friends, one of my closer friends, Jimmy Cumberland, included. We had a big group, about ten of us, racing down the rocky road and dirt paths that led us to the center of our imaginations.

Football in hand, we threw it back and forth, tossing it into the air and playfully teasing one another when one of us failed to catch it. We had a great plan for a game. It was to be some type of made-up sport, this combination between baseball and football. It was early February, so the air was cold, and the breeze bit our skin with its icy teeth, but that made no difference to us.

Partway into our journey, while sneaking under a chain-link fence, small flakes swished through the winter winds and fell from the heavy, white clouds. We got down to the cemetery, and I went out for a long pass; my friend Henry Benson launched one high and deep. I raced and saw the ball well, but it landed just out of my reach and bounced awkwardly into the woods. Naturally I scurried after it, but, with just the right amount of luck, it rolled to a stop next to a group of people with whom my friends and I didn't do much talking—girls. At ten and eleven years old, we were at that awkward age where girls aren't disgusting, but we still acted mean to them out of some misunderstood discomfort.

For me, however, I was slowly evolving from that uncomfortable stage, specifically with one girl. And, as fate would have it, there she was: Carrie Cassidy. Her light hair floated in the breeze and was decorated with small flashes of white from the flakes. Her blue eyes slowly turned toward the football that rested at her feet and then easily searched around until they met my frozen body just a few yards away.

"Is this yours?" Her soft voice whispered.

"Yes," I managed. I searched myself for some sign of courage and eventually found it buried beneath my flannel shirt and heavy jacket. I strutted up to the location of the ball and proceeded to lean forward and accept the football from her hands. "Thank you."

I began to walk away to return to the excitement of my anxious friends. So many things came to mind about what I could've said, what I should've said. I imagined myself turning around and speaking in some deep voice a very romantic line, but a shy reserve conquered my courage, and I went into a sprint, returning to where my friends continued their jokes. Little did I know, Carrie and I were destined for a story that would test the purity of that small second in our childhood, one that would evolve from the passion of our innocence, only to be tested by the incongruities of life.

Still, the day went on and the games continued until later that evening, when the approaching darkness signaled it was time to go home.

I took my usual route back, slipping under the fence and darting through my neighbors' yards. However, I heard something strange about four blocks from home. What I would then see would scar my heart and serve as my ever-present memory, my most honest image of the depression.

Jimmy lived in a small, simple house down the street. As he was about the same age, with about the same interests and ambitions, his dad too worked in the same mines as my father. However, after the stock market crash in '29, the mining business they worked for lost a large chunk of cash—as every business encountered. The financial deficit, naturally, eventually trickled down to the blue-collar level, and cuts were made. That day, Jimmy's father lost his job.

Ordinarily, I'm no peeping tom, but what I heard, for whatever reason, caught my attention.

At first, it was just the deep, booming voice of Mr. Cumberland. Filled with an anger unlike I had ever heard, his profanity cut through the frigid air like swords and stopped me in my tracks. I found myself strangely intrigued with curiosity as his voice bellowed against the wind. I snuck behind Jimmy's house and peered through a small hole in the corner of the back window. I saw Mr. Cumberland red with frustration.

"What is this crap? Why do we eat this crap every night? Can't you cook anything, you woman?" His words seemed to cut into the heart of Mrs. Cumberland with ferocious velocity.

"Baby, we are going to be okay," she managed, her eyes filled with tenderness, begging for mercy from her rampaging husband.

"Baby? Don't call me baby!" In one quick, fluid motion, he threw his plate directly towards her. The plate crashed against the wall behind her and rained over her head. Mrs. Cumberland shook with fear.

"Why are you doing this?" she pleaded, her voice filled with pain as she fell to her knees. Her hands began to bleed as they crashed against the shattered glass plates.

"'Cause we're not going to be okay! I lost my job, and we were barely getting by when I had one. You can't work, because if there is no job for a man, there certainly won't be one for a woman! Don't you get it? We have no money, we have no food, and soon we will have no house! I failed you. I failed Jimmy. I... I failed myself!"

Mrs. Cumberland glanced up, and her eyes met mine at the corner of the window. I had never met her, despite my friendship with Jimmy, but in that moment I swore I saw her whole life.

It is amazing the moments we witness. I ran home after that, my heart torn and sore with compassion. Still, my life went on. My dad kept his job, and my world continued to go round. For Mrs. Cumberland, however, that moment defined the end of an era in her life. Mr. Cumberland left for the bar that night and got drunk. He searched for a job for three weeks but eventually hopped on a train and never returned. Grief stricken, Mrs. Cumberland committed suicide three months later. Jimmy and his younger brother had no place to go. I don't know what happened to them, but after their mother's death, I never saw him again.

To me, they faded into nothingness. I saw that one moment in my life come and go and become a memory. I shared the most dramatic moment of their lives, and then for me it was gone. But for them, that moment lasted forever.

And life for me did go on. I played baseball throughout my adolescence, and my relationship with Carrie also continued to grow. We went on dates in middle school, formals in high school, and to carnivals during the summer. That small second of innocence in the cemetery had expanded from a single moment to fill every hour of our days, every cell of our hearts, every breath of our spirits. It had evolved from a quick, meaningless interaction into a relationship draped in purity.

I remember being twenty years old. It was 1938, the Great Depression still suppressed the nation but would come to a close some years later after we entered the war. I was smart, but more than that, I was intellectual. I would read the Bible. I would contemplate life, death, and whatever else was destined to follow. I thought I was special; I thought I was a different breed of man, unique to my generation, unique to the world, some sort of Gandhi or Buddha.

I remember taking walks into the woods on Sunday afternoons, just after church. I would skip rocks across the river and stare at the deep, blue sky, imagining what lay beyond the borders of the horizon. Lying next to Carrie, I would watch the trees dance in the breeze and listen to the birds sing as they skated across the sky on nothing but air.

"How would you define God?" I would ask Carrie as she smiled and giggled at my questions.

"I'm serious," I would say with a smile and tickle her side just to see her laugh again. "Is he some old man, just sitting up there on the clouds with a big beard and heavy heart? Or is he something more abstract? Does he love or is he love...? I just...I don't know."

She would stroke my chest and just keep smiling.

"You know," she'd start. "I think maybe he is both at the same time. Maybe he is physical in our minds just so we have something tangible that we can touch with our hands. But maybe, maybe he is some ever-present spirit breathing inside our hearts, training our compassion, teaching us to love."

"You know?" I'd smile. "I don't think we'll ever know."

Then I would quickly turn and grab her side. She'd scream and get up, diving into the water. I swear we were the one beautiful thing in that whole town during that time.

I thought we were one of a kind, deeper than the water we swam in. Maybe we were; but about thirty years later I took a walk. I walked through the same trees, walked along the same river, let my thoughts race around my head and tie my emotions into knots. Everything exactly the same, Carrie hand in hand next to me, our relationship matured by mistakes, pain, and troubles but still alive through the strength of love.

We came up to the spot where we shared our Sunday afternoons. However, as we approached, we heard a familiar giggle from the bushes. We stealthily crept behind a tree, and what we saw amazed me.

We saw ourselves from forty years before—youth and old age united through generations, the barrier of time fallen for at least a few moments. We saw the young man cradle her slender body between his strong arms, cradling not only her body but her whole heart. We saw them share a quiet smile, a deep thought, a quick kiss. They balanced on a beam of fragile, young love.

I turned to Carrie and stared into her eyes, just as they did, just as we had years before. And there we stood, young and old love, young and old bodies, two generations simultaneously encountering the same cycle of life. Each special, each unique, but still each the same. It was the most amazing thing I had ever seen.

It was then I realized something very interesting about life. Just when you think you have found yourself in some unknown territory, just when you think you have experienced something never before heard of, in reality you are only one tiny particle of history, pioneering the same emotions, ideas, and experiences of a generation before and a generation later.

Carrie's and my love, our thoughts, our intellectual explorations were special. In the book of our lives, it was new, exciting, and beautiful. But in the end we are all part of some greater cycle, some greater process. We are all united somehow; time is just our way of defining that relationship.

Carrie's and my love continued to flourish over the next few years. We never stopped swimming through the depths of our desires, and soon eternity would be ours, or so it appeared. But when I was twenty-three years old, life proved to us for the first time that nothing ever goes according to plan—the United States was attacked. The nation was shaken as our confident president lead us into modern hell—World War II. It was one of those things that happen, but you are never really able to grip your head or heart around, like some nightmare that tortures your imagination but couldn't possibly be real.

But it was real. It was more real than anything that had ever happened. It was as real as the depression, as real as the tears that drowned the broken dreams and vanished futures of those who were killed on that infamous day.

It's weird how it was those tears, however, that became the glue of our nation. We followed our president into war with our hearts glowing, prepared to be brave. Ten days after December 7, 1941, I enlisted in the army, leaving behind the mines I had found myself suppressed in for five years. This was my calling to greatness—maybe I wouldn't play for the Pirates, but I still saw my destiny as some beautiful star, and Japan was the big dipper.

Before I was going to be sent into any combat, much to my disappointment, I had to endure some military training. I was sent to Georgia to go through somewhat of a boot camp, to learn how to be a real American soldier. My drill sergeant was Sergeant Jason Smith, and he was the most intense man I had ever met.

"McNamy!" he would scream. "Get your fat butt in line, you piece of crap!"

I never thought I would miss the mines.

"Move! Those Japs will tag your butt if you don't learn how to fight like a real man, McNamy! We are American soldiers! Let's go!" Smith's intensity, to say the least, was harsh, but still there was something inspiring in his tone and speech. He made me want to be the best soldier to

Threads of Truth

walk the earth; he made me remember why I was there, why I enlisted, why this was where I needed to be. His passion for winning that war was contagious.

All in all, boot camp was not bad. I had the opportunity to build a second family within my unit of the battalion, and I knew if all else failed, I was willing to die for those men I met. Jimmy Simpson, Tyler Mason, Jackson Bailey, Patrick O'Neil, Emilio Camillo, and many more were not the most perfect of men I ever met, but they were certainly the closest to brothers I ever had.

In August of 1942 we said good-bye to Sergeant Smith and were deployed to some islands in the middle of the Pacific. I can't honestly say I knew where we were, and I probably couldn't find it on a map, but that defined my experience in the war—confused and lost but burning to do something great. It didn't take me long, however, to learn that war was not the birthplace of greatness. Bravery was not for your country but for yourself and your comrades.

Within the first weeks of our deployment we faced our first adversity. In the jungles of whatever island we were on, we encountered Japanese resistance. It was not at all the glorifying experience I had dreamed of.

Mortars lit up the sky like fireworks, and bullets hummed passed our ears like some pissed off bumble bee. The crowded forest played tricks on our eyes, and consequently our sanity. My gun shook in my hands as I swallowed fear like a sharp rock. Occasionally I closed my eyes to escape the torture, but I would only wake up seconds later to meet it face-to-face once again. I searched deep inside myself to find that hidden courage I had dreamed of so many nights. I dug through the thick layers of self-doubt, fear, and, most of all, sanity, to find some type of reckless bravery. That is what bravery truly is; the ability to swallow fear and forget sanity. It is the ability to do what is completely crazy in the face of danger.

I said a quick prayer and turned on my stomach into the foreboding jungle. To my left, Patrick O'Neil squealed as a bullet hissed straight through his abdomen. My mind burned with rage at the sight of my dying friend, and I fired off a series of shots. To my right, a crew of four or five progressed forward and horizontally to try and wrap around to the flank of the Japanese unit. Out there, there was no organized warfare, however. This was guerilla warfare—chaotic and confusing. I saw what looked like a natural bunker about fifteen yards ahead of me and charged full speed toward it. In my sprint, a bullet clipped my left arm; I screamed in agony as I leaped into the small crater. My voice echoed throughout the hallways of the jungle.

As I hit the ground, I turned to my right and saw a Jap there who had obviously had the same idea. He immediately whipped out a pistol but somehow misfired and hit me in the leg. Unable to grab my own pistol, I jumped on him and began to whale. He yelped and shouted something in Japanese. I told him to shut the hell up and then reached for my knife. I reared back and pounded his face repeatedly. He came back and jabbed me in the side. I felt a piercing pain shoot through my oblique and down my leg, racing through my entire body like some fire on a line of gasoline.

I then took my knife and stabbed his neck with all the might I could muster. He dropped his knife as all intensity left his eyes.

Suddenly I was staring into the face of another man. In the tenderness of his eyes in those last few moments I saw he too had a story. He probably had a wife and children and had probably come to war with the same hopeful heart of a glorified and honorable destiny.

When he was in that bunker he too encountered the same emotions of fear and journeyed on the same internal struggle for courage. He had fought, just as I, for what he saw as righteous, what he saw as good. Neither of us fought in vain. I then began to cry as the battle around us came to a quiet close. War no longer made sense to me.

Despite my emotional breakdown, I continued on an island-hopping journey through the pacific for the next couple years. I killed many more men. I brought an end to the stories of many men who attempted to do the same to me. It was then that I learned that the true root of evil is not in the man or the institution that you attempt to annihilate but is rather found in the act of killing itself. I may have murdered a sinful man, but I too, am a sinful man—yet neither of us is evil. At that point in my life I called evil Satan, and somewhere in the middle of the Pacific I learned that Satan was not in my enemy but in the animosity between us.

When I was ten years old I played war with pots as helmets and sticks as guns, thinking I was to be some hero out on that battlefield and inspired by the modesty of those who were dubbed true war heroes. But now I understand that their humility is a result of knowing the real truth.

Out there, on that battlefield, there are no heroes. There are survivors and there are the dead. All those men would rather be dead, because that is where the glory really lies.

Three weeks after that first encounter with the Japanese, we met again in Southeast Asia on another jungle-infested island. It was the deadliest battle I fought over my term in the war.

The stench of death drowned the warm, October, pacific air, and fear gripped the hearts of all. Bullets spontaneously whispered through the air and elicited a quick, painful yelp. The battle was slow but steady and lasted nearly five days. The surreal quietness could drive a man crazy—if you weren't already.

Mosquitoes provided for a second enemy, and even the safest of bunkers left a naked and exposed feeling torturing your sanity.

For the entire battle I hid, scared and clueless. I watched several friends die, and I let them bleed. I was a coward, and every time I see my purple heart of bravery hanging from my old uniform I remember that battle. I was no hero, I just survived—that was my only victory.

War was not all a battle of cowards, however. I must not omit the scenes of uninhibited bravery I saw.

Jason Brownley dove on a grenade to save the lives of three men. Ross Peterson sacrificed his life to avoid a conflict by diverting a Japanese brigade. Ryan Calbert carried a man on his back for half a mile to save his life.

These stories and many more touched my heart, and I will never forget them. Only a few men were blessed with the ability to express this rare and pure courage but by doing so inspired me to do my part in surviving. They were my stars in the middle of a dark storm—to say it simply, those men were my one and only mark of hope during that war.

I came home from the war in July of '45. I came home, and the nation was changed. Towns that had suffered began to prosper, men without jobs had them, families without money made some. It was as if the world's suffering caused some reverse effect back home.

All the while, Carrie waited for me. She worked while I fought, and we had written each other regularly. We exchanged love letters, funny stories, and fake promises that things were okay and that I would soon be home—but then again, sometimes the truth doesn't matter. Sometimes you have to make your own reality to feel like you have something to fight for. And as it turns out, we picked up right where we left off.

We suspended our love for three years and dove back into the water, laughing like life had restored its purity.

Outside the McNamy house the sun's fiery tongues stuck to the sky. The blue atmosphere slowly melted into darkness.

Inside, the tears dimmed as reality began to grip their hearts. Life slowly oozed from his mouth in a series of random, cold breaths. As time wisped through his mind, it slowly ticked on the walls of the room, keeping pace with the sinking sun.

I remember being a grown man. I was twenty-eight years old, I asked Carrie to marry me, and she said yes. The ship of my life sailed into a bright future. I wrote books on the lives of fictional characters, but simultaneously I filled the pages of my own life. My dreams had matured from a professional baseball player to a professional dad, a great husband, a better Christian.

I remember talking with Carrie late at night, playing out the rest of our lives in our imaginations, feeding our hopeful hearts with prayers for the future. We had been destined for happiness since the age of ten, and forever had finally begun for us. The thing about life, though, is that plans mean nothing. We draw our fate across our hearts and pray for reality to accept those dreams. And in the end, it almost never does.

We moved to New Jersey after we married to get as far from the mines as we could afford. It was a small house, with a stove and three rooms on each of two floors; but it was cheap, and it was what the army gave us for my service. Carrie was a riveter during the war and tried to stay in the work world after V.E. Day and I had come home. Still, with so many returning men, women seemed to return to what was accepted as their hemisphere—the house. I wrote in my free time with the aspirations of becoming a writer. Still, I searched for a job to make a living until I broke through.

One day in particular proved pivotal in the turning of our plans, however.

It was an average night; the sun had just set, but remnants of its rays still slightly lit the sky under a peaceful blue. I was returning home, traveling along the highway toward the suburbia in which we lived—one of those small towns where all the houses looked the same, with a small picket fence around the front and a grill in the back.

I had been unsuccessful in my quest for work, regretting my lack of a college education. Still, I remained optimistic.

On the drive home, however, there was a certain turn, after the exit from the highway, where the softly lit sky seemed to play tricks on your eyes. You would always think you'd see the fading shadow of an oncoming car, but it tended to be just the swift flash of your own car bending around the dimming rays of the sun. I pulled up to that turn, restless and eager to see Carrie. I saw the shadow but quickly ignored it and accelerated into the turn.

There was a large crash as my car skidded across the parkway and smashed against the curb. My vehicle swerved then rolled; my body felt like a feather in the wind. I remember a burning sensation absorbing my body, a piercing pain jolting into my leg, and then all went black.

I woke up an hour later in a hospital.

Doctors were the first thing I saw. They were circled around my head with a giant head light at the center, blasting into my face. At first my eyes frantically searched their faces but eventually restlessly closed. I didn't feel or see anything for the rest of the time they operated, but I heard bits and pieces of scattered comments—of which only some I understood.

"His ribs are shattered," I heard a voice say at one point.

"We might have to amputate," I then heard after what seemed like ten minutes but in reality was about one and a half hours. I dipped in and out of consciousness like an ebbing tide on unsure waters.

The first thing I felt after the accident was fear and uncertainty. Then I felt a piercing pain in my left leg and a burning sensation in the right side of my face. I managed to turn my head to see my left arm limp in a bandage. I tried to move it but couldn't. Then the fear came again.

I had fought in a war and emerged physically stable. Now I was home, I was safe, and I felt as though some Kraut or Jap had just thrown a grenade in my foxhole.

My father had always taught me to be tough; crying was a weakness. But right then, I cried. Tears drowned my spirit as my faith began to dwindle in the grasp of the doctors operating on me.

"Why?" I would scream out to the heavens with a doubtful heart and a questioning soul. "Why, Jesus? What have I done?"

Nothing made sense. I was a good man. I was a Christian. I was a believer, but he chose to persecute me! Millions of murderers, criminals, and robbers ran loose and prospered through their corruption. But not me. I sat there with my morals as tightly wrapped around my life as the bandages that held my arm together.

The next four months in that hospital changed my life. Not because I would heal and rediscover my original faith. But because I would meet many people, two in particular, who would open my eyes and heart to a new perspective.

The first one was my doctor—the voice I heard during those hours of surgery. Dr. Mitchell was an atheist, but I swear he was also an angel. I finally met him two weeks after the accident, and I will never forget our conversation.

"Hello, Mr. McNamy, my name is Dr. Mitchell. I operated on you after the accident."

"Oh, oh man, s-sir," I stuttered, "I'm n-not exactly sure what to s-say."

"Don't say anything. Just get better for me," he replied, proud yet humble.

"Just, I guess... well, just t-thank God for you, sir," I managed.

"No. Thank Dr. Andrews," he quickly said, turning to walk out of the room.

I looked at him. "Who's that?" I asked, overcome by my curiosity.

Dr. Mitchell stopped and turned his head.

"He is the doctor who taught me the operation I performed on you." He smiled. "Without him, you wouldn't be here." He then proceeded out of the room.

I lay there completely perplexed. I had never met a man who doubted or even dared to question God, and here was a man who told me it was not God, but Dr. Andrews, who was the reason for my existence at that moment.

One month later, I met the next most influential man in my journey toward discovering my faith. He was a Muslim, and his name was Abikahr Hussan.

Abikahr had cancerous tumors near his heart and had already had two operations to remove the tumors each time they returned. After his surgery, he was placed in the same room as me for recovery.

He must've heard me late one night, damning my guardian angel under my breath, whispering against the window as I stared into space.

"You know, for a man who wears a cross on his heart, you sure hate your God," he stated out of the blue one day.

Shocked and frustrated by the comment, I hesitated but shot back, "Yeah, well, for a God who is supposed to merciful, he sure has been relentless with me."

"What? You think he did this to you?"

"Well, he sure didn't do anything to stop it."

"You American Christians. What does faith mean to you? A pretty necklace you wear on Sundays?"

Now I'd had it. Anger boiled in my stomach. Who did this Muhammad want-to-be think he was? My pride was hurt. He didn't know me; he didn't know about my Sunday afternoons, my deep thoughts, my deep passion for truth.

"Why don't you go screw yourself."

"Yep. You're only skin deep; one laceration, one bruise, and what you really believe leaks out with your blood."

"And why don't you tell me what you think that is?"

"Nothing. Not even you know what that is. That is the point."

Threads of Truth

"Oh, yeah? Well, what do you believe? Allah, Muhammad, and all that horse crap?"

"Well, to a point, yes. But that isn't what my faith is in."

"Well what, then?"

"Love, compassion, and peace. I have faith in all of these things, and I believe they are in all people. Like a light suppressed by anger, hunger for vengeance, but mostly fear."

I was stunned. He rolled over and went to sleep. I sat in silence, staring at the ceiling for the rest of the day.

The next day I heard Abikahr's story. I was blown away.

There I sat with my beautiful past and my promising future. I was about to lose, physically, one to two years of my life, and then I would return to normalcy; his life was crippled by sadness, illness, and was constantly balancing on a thin line of uncertainty. Ordinarily I would have attributed this to his misplaced faith, some sort of punishment or hint from God—but suddenly, I hesitated.

My faith was not redirected; I will always love Jesus Christ, and he will always worship Allah. But in that hospital room, I learned there was really no difference in our faith. Faith is not the history we study but the lifestyle we preach, the actions we encourage. Yes, he was a Muslim; yes, I am a Christian, but when I listened to him, when I stared into the depths of his faith, I saw myself.

I came to believe in the light I saw in other people. I came to believe that that light was God. I no longer envisioned some Santa Claus figure studying me from the stars, listening to my prayers—God was something much more abstract.

God, to me, is a piece of each and every one of us. He is some beauty inside us, the love and compassion between us. To be saved is not to worship Him under the same name as I call Him; to be saved is to love with the same passion that He loves us.

Call Him Allah, call Him Brahma and Vishnu, call Him Yahweh—but more importantly, listen to Him. Learn to love, learn to have faith in people, learn to have faith in yourself, and never stop believing in that good. It is always there, in everyone.

I was there the day after Abikahr's surgery. He didn't make it. He died, and his memory faded into time, but he left me with this gift.

I remember the day he died very clearly. I remember Dr. Mitchell walking into the room with a pair of nurses—they folded new sheets across his bed and prepared for the next patient. I remember the pain in Dr. Mitchell's eyes as he cleared and cleaned the area where Abikahr had spent his final waking moments.

"What happened?" I asked courageously but already knowing.

"I lost him."

I was silent as I watched Dr. Mitchell burst into tears. At first I couldn't believe it as this professional, who had surely "lost" lives before, broke down right in front of me.

"Doc, I'm sure you did what you could."

"I'm not crying for me. I'm crying for him."

Again there was silence. This time, however, he got up quickly and headed for the door.

"Why did you become a doctor?" I quickly asked.

"It's what I've wanted to do since I was eight. My dad died of cancer. I decided I wanted to save people from that pain. I thought I could. I thought I could play God."

"No one can be God."

"Nope. Not even God can. That is why we have doctors." He exited the room, but within seconds he returned.

"I'm a doctor because somebody has to look out for the good in the world. So many people lose faith in life at the first sign of chaos. I try and keep a faith in living by saving lives. I feel like there is a battle between me and death, and he won today."

I just stared at him as he again took off down the hallway. At that moment I felt like I had two guardian angels—Jesus Christ and Dr. Mitchell.

Just as I had fought in the war, I now fought a physical and spiritual battle against myself. And through it all, Carrie waited. She was—I won't be cliché and say a "tower of strength"—a constant reminder of my dreams through some of the darkest times of my life. Yet somehow, those darkest times were in many ways the most beautiful.

In any case, I recovered from my physical disabilities through months of rehabilitation and after a year of crippling pain.

I remember working with a trainer, trying to re-strengthen every muscle in the left side of my body, and

I remember looking up to see my wonderful wife sitting there with a smile of encouragement. She was frozen in time; she had delayed her life, or so it seemed, until I could fully regain mine. That kind of graceful endurance pulled me through, I think, just as much as my prayers and trainer.

I was thirty years old in August of 1948, the month in which the second half of my life began. I finished up my last day of my rehabilitation, and Carrie and I celebrated with dinner. It was a wonderful night.

After dinner we returned home, happy as ever—which I must admit was partially induced by beverage—but still, it felt as pure as anything. We stumbled into our bedroom, and I felt her slender, beautiful, and angelic body in my rusty, battered, yet powerful, arms. The night carried us into heaven.

About a month later, Carrie announced to me her pregnancy.

"I missed," she said awkwardly.

"Missed what?"

"Umm...w-well..." She stuttered and bit her lower lip, her eyes glistening with disbelief but excitement.

"What? Carrie, what happened?"

"Hey, daddy," she said with a giggle.

I honestly believe my heart leapt from my chest at that moment. This is no metaphor; my heart literally jumped through the dungeon of my chest and dove through her soft skin, then nestled up next to what would become my baby girl eight months later. It would remain with her for the rest of my life and the rest of hers—though she didn't always know it.

Threads of Truth

On May 17, 1949, Peyton Shiloh McNamy entered this world.

Having a child awakens some other type of love in your soul. Some deep passion that had until then been hidden in the corners of your imagination. Peyton became the center of my joy; more than that, she became my joy itself. I always loved Carrie, and I always will, but there is something so indescribably miraculous about having a child. You look down at the purity of their wide and curious eyes, and all you can do is smile. You know they will grow up and will do great things, or maybe they will do nothing, but to you they are always that beautiful child, with those big, passionate eyes, yearning for life. Sure, I knew Peyton would grow up, I knew she would date, fall in love, have a kid. I knew she would mess up, fall apart, break down, and cry. But no matter what, she was always going to be my joy.

I found a small, temporary job working at a local firm. I played the role similar to that of a secretary. I just needed to make some money until I could find something else. In my free time, I wrote.

I wrote about anything and everything. To me, that was the beautiful thing about writing. There were no rules—just raw emotion, poured through the thin, plastic lining of a pen, scattered across the page in random patterns of ink to form some meaning, any meaning, or, sometimes, no meaning.

I wrote about life. Mostly, I wrote about my life, the lives of those I witnessed, the lives of those I dreamed to live. I would stretch my mind to find the borders of my imagination, and in my dreams I clung to some ever-present hope that I would one day be considered a great writer. It was a boyish hope, the same thing that endorsed my childhood aspirations and allowed me to work hard and constantly push myself. I would talk about this dream to those around me, but most people just laughed. I know behind my back they joked and teased. It never bothered me. That hope may seem childish, but to me hope is the only thing we depend on to survive sometimes. Sometimes we lose everything, and the only thing we have is a battered heart, willing to endure.

That is, in some ways, what Peyton would always be to me as well—hope. If I messed up, she was my chance to fix things; if I was wrong, she was my chance to be right. She was my best foot forward, and if all else failed, I still had her.

So I chose to combine my two prayers for greatness. I wrote about Peyton.

I was forty-four in 1962. Peyton turned thirteen years old that May, and Carrie was forty-three. I had finally found a steady job working at the bank. Life was picture perfect.

But just when we think we have found ourselves somewhere comfortable, life throws us a curveball. I swung and missed.

Susan Bennet was a beautiful woman. She had long, silky, blonde hair, a charming smile, and enchanting green eyes.

Now, I was happily married and had been deeply in love with Carrie since my childhood, but there was a mysterious sensuality to Susan that caught hold of me. I told myself to ignore it, to let it go; but my body burned with curiosity at the sight of her, and on July 4, 1962, I made the biggest mistake of my life.

"Hey, Brian," Susie greeted me with that mystifying grin. "What are you doing here? The bank is closed today, isn't it?"

"Oh how ya' doin,' Suz? Yeah it is. I just forgot some stuff. Had to come in and get it today. What about you? I am sure you have got some fun plans for Independence Day."

"Actually, no. I usually go home to Pennsylvania for holidays, but I decided to just stay in town. I have only lived here for a few weeks, and I am still getting to know everybody. I don't really have any plans, though."

"I see, yeah. Carrie, Peyton, and I were just going to have a cookout on the grill with some neighbors. You are welcome to come."

"Really? That's so sweet of you. Sure, that... um, that sounds great. Where exactly do you live?"

"Oh, you can just follow me. It's 'bout five minutes from here. Not far at all." As I picked up a box filled with some files I wanted to look over on the weekend, it slipped through my fingers and hit my foot with a thud. I hopped for a second to shake out the pain then proceeded to slide on a chair I attempted to lean on and thunked my head against a desk. I blacked out. A complete freak accident that I'm sure looked comical from an outsider's perspective.

I woke up, from what Susan told me, about ten minutes later. I opened my eyes to see Susan still smiling down at me, holding a pack of ice—probably retrieved from the freezer behind the office—to my head. Her face glistened under the lights; her blouse parted mid-way down her chest. I couldn't do anything but smile back. We broke out laughing.

"Well, this is embarrassing," I commented with a blush.

She laughed. "It's okay; you're cute enough to pull off the clumsy act."

What followed was an awkward moment in which we both smiled sheepishly, as if two teenagers with small crushes. The ice slipped from her hand.

"Whoops!" She chuckled. She leaned down to pick up the ice. I smelled her sweet perfume. As she neared my face, our eyes met once again.

Next thing I knew, our lips were locked in a beautiful moment of bliss. Passion surged from our mouths.

And so the demise of my perfect life began, or so it seemed. One afternoon, one mistake, one submission to my darkest desires, and I threw away anything good I had ever done for or with the one whom I had always called my one true love.

The party was weird. Susan and I shared awkward smiles across the backyard, and Carrie constantly stroked my back, wondering if something was wrong. She had so much tenderness in her, so much compassion. It killed me to know I scarred that part of her. I am a permanent bruise on what was her most pure trait. I discolored her innocence and am her constant reminder that life never goes according to plan.

The affair between Susan and I continued for the better part of the remaining months of 1962. Over and over again I submitted myself to my irrepressible desires, each time allowing them to escalate. Carrie never knew.

Come Christmas, guilt cornered my hidden conscience. I told Susan I had to bring an end to our romance, and she willingly agreed, obviously bothered by the same restless anxiety. I told Carrie on December 22.

I walked in the door, dragging my legs, along with my pride, behind me.

"What's wrong, baby?" Carrie asked so affectionately, in that sweet, innocent tone. I was dying inside.

"There is ... uh, there is somethin' I gotta tell you."

"Of course, love. What is it?"

"Take a seat."

"Why?"

"Just take a seat."

She slowly eased herself onto the couch, never breaking eye contact.

I paused for a moment as my mind turned, playing out different scenarios in my head, different ways to tell her. Nothing sounded right.

"For the past five or six months I have been having an affair with Susan Bennet from the office." I broke down into tears.

Her eyes went blank. They were dead, as if my words were a black hole of pain, sucking away all her life. I reached out to touch her hand, but she slowly pulled away.

She did not look at me, would never look at me, the same. Her eyes remained wide as she stood up and walked out the door. Five minutes later Peyton came out from her room. There she was—my marker of hope. She approached the couch and said nothing. She had heard through the door. Her eyes were red from tears, the blood of her broken spirit, and she needed comfort, just as I. She was angry, I could tell, but for now we faced something greater than guilt. We stared into the face of our family's anguish, and we both, to say it simply, needed a hug.

Six months after that emotional night, Carrie filed the divorce papers. I again began to cry when I saw them and put them off for about a month. That same month, my life's decline grew more painful—both my parents died in an accident.

I had not seen or talked to either of my sisters in a decade, and at the funeral nothing much changed. I said my good-byes, but my emotions choked every word that bubbled up through my throat. At forty-five years old, I faced the reality that I was entirely alone in this world. My wife had left me, my parents had died, and my siblings had detached themselves. I had what seemed like one chance to do things right, and that was as a father.

As a teenager, Peyton got a little into the counter-culture movement of the '60s, which in some ways helped her grow more accepting of my mistake, but in other ways made the task of parenting and taming her wild approach to life much more difficult. Still, she was so beautiful, and every day she grew more and more like her mother. But Peyton was not always with me, and when she wasn't, my sanity was tortured by guilt, anger, and sadness. I would remember how perfect my life once seemed, how beautiful. My future seemed so bright, so wonderful. And now, there I stood, a forty-eight-year-old man alone in his dark house, robbed by his own mistakes and by the oscillations of life, robbed of all the love he once embraced.

It was the saddest time of my life.

In their will, my parents left me their house in Pennsylvania. I moved in during January of 1965. By that time, Carrie's and my divorce was official, and so was my solitude.

I saw Peyton for every other holiday and for six weeks during the summer. Carrie had custody of her the rest of the time. My seclusion, however painful, gave me the privacy necessary to reflect and truly start my novel.

It was a refreshing experience to return home. Although the town had evolved over the years, much was still the same. I would walk down to the cemetery and remember shooting my BB gun; I would sit by the baseball field and allow my memories to carry me back to my childhood dreams. I remembered playing catch, pretending to be the shortstop for the Pirates, the Yankees, the Reds—whoever I was to sign with. I wondered where those childhood dreams had gone. And so I wrote.

I wrote about dreams; I wrote about hope, about memories, about growing up, and about messing up. With Peyton as my inspiration, I filled 236 pages with the most beautiful words I had ever spoken, written, read, or dreamt of.

And finally, after forty-five years of dreaming, twenty years of planning, and five years of writing, I published a book in the spring of 1970. I was fifty-two years old, and

I thought I was at last leaving my mark of greatness on this earth. I imagined millions of people reading my book, and my words leaping from the page, landing solidly on the lives of all those within reach. The power of my words nestled softly in the hearts of millions. I had accomplished what I thought was my truest greatness.

Still, my life felt empty.

I begged Carrie to come and visit me. Peyton was twenty-two years old and mapping out her own life, just as her mother and I had thirty years before. If she were to visit, it would be only her and me. One can imagine she was hesitant.

By some miracle, she still agreed to come.

We went out to eat at a local, small-town restaurant, the only lasting business from our childhood, and now one of our old friends was the owner. The meal was slightly awkward as we shared "How are yous" and "What have you been up tos," but I just couldn't believe she was there and was perpetually thankful for it.

She stayed with her sister, who had never left our hometown, but the next day we went on a walk.

"Do you remember when we used to walk through here?"

"Yeah." She smiled softly, sharing the memory.

"And we would chase each other around, both of us acting like we were trying to escape but secretly wishing for the other's skin to brush against ours." I laughed, but she still kept her smile a secret, as if trying to hold it back.

"You know things will never be the same, Brian." She was blunt.

"I know, and we will never be sixteen again. I don't want them to be the same."

"Brian, it has been seven or eight or... it's been almost a decade. You can't just call me up and invite me over, tell a few stories, and expect us to just pick up where we left off. It hurt, Brian. It still hurts and it always will. We need to move on."

"Carrie—"

"Look, Brian, you wrote your book. You're doing well; I am doing fine. Why are we here?"

"Because I wanted to see you. I miss you."

"Why?"

"Because it's been years, and I miss you!"

"*No*! Why did you do it?"

"I don't know! Some stupid curiosity. Some unexplainable desire. I gave in. I was weak! I'm sorry. I wish I could change the past. I wish things could be the same, but I know they won't."

"So let's move on. We will never be together again."

"I still love you, and I know somewhere inside of you, you love me too."

She paused. Tears soaked her skin, just as the last time I had talked to her about something other than custody or divorce.

"I'm not asking to get married. I'm not asking for anything. I just want to be with you, because I am getting older, and I want to be with the one I love. Please!"

The moment was suspended in time. Her tear-filled eyes met mine, and I know she saw the same thing I did. A childhood romance, a powerful compassion that pulls through injury, a broken marriage—but still, through it all, above anything, a pure, true love.

Without any words, we walked forward. I reached for her hand, and she unexpectedly embraced mine. Another mile down the path we saw a couple just like our younger selves. Giggling and swimming through the water. We both smiled at each other. We both knew.

Carrie permanently moved back to Pennsylvania. She didn't live with me for another few years, and things *weren't* the same, but they were beautiful in a different way. Our love had become a survival story.

I told Carrie one day when we were both about sixty years old, sitting on our front balcony, that I didn't know why she forgave me, but I was glad she did.

"Forgiving was the easy part," she said. "It was coming to grips with what had happened and then readjusting my life and my future that was hard."

"But why? How could forgiving possibly be easy? It makes no sense that you would forgive me." My curiosity again got the best of me. But she said nothing.

I eventually figured that was the point. Mercy makes no sense, but that is what is so unmistakably beautiful about it.

When I was sixty-three and Peyton was thirty-two, she got married. That was the most wonderful and most difficult experience of my life. To see my baby girl all dressed in white, her gorgeous gown draped across her slender body, a magical glow emanating from her smile—she was an angel. That was the wonderful part, but as I walked her down the aisle and looked into her gleaming eyes, I realized she had become more than just my beautiful little angel; she had become a woman. And as I gave her away, I realized I was letting go of my baby girl, releasing her from the warmth of my heart to let her fall into the arms of another.

Of course I would always be there for her, but I would no longer be the one she would always turn to. I was the second-string man in her life, and I had to adjust.

Her fiancé was a wonderful man, however, and the ceremony couldn't have been more perfect. And although I recognized all of this as I watched her say her vows, I couldn't help but think she was still the center of my joy, with those big, pure and innocent eyes; those small, warm arms; and that beautiful, tender heart. She was, and always would be, my baby girl.

A heart attack and a decade later, time had finally worn me down. I sat on my deathbed, surrounded by doctors, priests, Carrie, and Peyton. I sat there, replaying my entire life, waiting—just waiting for my heart to stop beating. Waiting for my final thought to pulse through my mind.

That's when it hit me. *Isn't it amazing?* I thought. It truly is amazing how one man's story, however ordinary or extraordinary, can fill the pages of a book. All the people, the experiences, the dreams, the mistakes, the triumphs—all of them, carefully woven together throughout our lives, working cohesively to bring us to wherever we end up. I do regret the mistake I made with Carrie, but had I not made it, who knows if I would have written my book or experienced the resurgence of a broken love. Sometimes you just have to trust life.

I suddenly realized my greatest accomplishment was not as a father, as a soldier, as a son, or as a writer. We spend our whole lives dreaming of when we will finally reach the pinnacle of our greatness, but it wasn't until those last few moments that I realized a man's greatness is found in the entirety of his life. Not a single experience, but all of them. It is the wisdom we take from them and the memories they give us that is truly great about life. It was those two things that I was left with in the end.

In those last few moments Brian McNamy relived his entire life. His loved ones slowly counted the seconds as time pulsed against the walls, yet in his restless mind, McNamy saw, witnessed, his entire life—his dreams, his failures, his triumphs, his mistakes. As his last breaths dripped from his chest and melted in the air, his memories raced wildly through his soul.

His life came to a close just as the day faded to night. And as his memories drifted into history, gliding on the wind of his final breath, family and friends mourned those last precious moments that seemed to last for an eternity. The beauty of a life, lost in the sails of time, and simultaneously the cycle of time carried another story into the future.

The sun has now set, and McNamy has now passed, but the world still goes round, only to wake the next morning to tell another story.